New B

(Second Chances Series #3)

New Beginnings

Second Chances Series, Volume 3

Morris Fenris

Published by Morris Fenris, 2021.

NEW BEGINNINGS

First edition. September 10, 2021.

Copyright © 2021 Morris Fenris.

ISBN: 978-1521219010

Written by Morris Fenris.

Morris Fenris

Prologue

Sometimes the darkest hour is simply the end of the tunnel just before sunrise. Tragedy can either break you or make you; the end result is up to you. And always remember, the sun will shine again. It may not be visible from where you are, but above the clouds, it *is* shining!

Chapter 1

San Diego, California, January 27th...

S   "Dani, if you don't hurry, you're going to be late for preschool," Grace hollered from the kitchen. She paused to listen for the sound of little feet coming down the hallway, frowning when all she heard was silence.

Putting the last clean plate back in the cupboard, she wiped her hands on a dishtowel as she went to investigate. "Dani?" she called, pushing the door to her daughter's bedroom open and looking around for her.

"Shush," came the whispered demand, and Grace looked around again, still not seeing her.

She crossed the bedroom, bending down to look under the bed. Still no little girl. "Dani? Where are you?" she whispered back.

"In the closet," came back the reply

Confused and growing slightly alarmed, Grace carefully opened the closet door, peeking around the corner as she did so, afraid of the mischief her four-year-old might have gotten into in the time between breakfast and getting dressed for school. *She's only been alone for fifteen minutes. Tops! Really, how much mischief could she have gotten into in that little amount of time?*

She pulled the door open a little further and felt her heart melt at the sight that greeted her. Dani had pulled the extra blankets down from the shelves, using her stepstool from the bathroom. The stool still sat in front of the shelves, tipped over on its side, and the blankets were piled around her little munchkin.

She had draped them haphazardly over the lower hanging rod in her closet, creating what she assumed was a four-year-olds version of a tent. Squatting down to look her daughter in the eye, she whispered, "What are you doing in here?"

Daniella had her body turned slightly away from her mother, and fidgeted before she answered, "I don't want to go to school today."

Grace looked at her, wondering what had changed between breakfast and her trek down the hall. She replayed the events quickly in her mind. Daniella had hurried through her breakfast, excited to get to school today because they were going to visit the butterfly house. She'd hollered about her missing rainbow-colored tennis shoes and Grace had told her they were on the back step...

She peered at her daughter again, noticing that her right hand seemed to be scratching something beneath the blanket. Giving Daniella a smile, she softly asked, "Dani, what have you got under there?"

Daniella got a mulish look on her face and turned to protect whatever was behind the blanket that was hanging down.

"Come on, now. Let momma see what you've found." Grace started to reach for the blanket, but Dani grabbed hold of her hand.

"No! You'll make her leave and she's mine."

Grace closed her eyes on a sigh and silently asked the Good Lord for patience. Opening her eyes, she took a breath and then calmly asked the million-dollar question. "Who and what is she?"

"I'm going to name her Arianna," Daniella told her mother, a glint in her eye that promised a tantrum of huge proportions if she didn't get her way.

"Arianna? And what kind of animal is Arianna?"

"Promise you won't make me get rid of her?" Daniella begged, batting her eyelashes and pushing her bottom lip out in a pout worthy of an Oscar.

"Honey, you know I can't do that. She might belong to someone else..."

"But, they didn't take care of her 'cuz she was lost. I won'ts ever lets her gets lost." Dani made a big production of drawing a big X-shape across her chest. "Please, can't I keep her?"

Why me? Grace searched for a soft voice and then stated, "Well, first things first. Why don't you come out of the closet and introduce me to your new friend?" Grace stood up and then, hearing a noise, looked to see Jane standing in the doorway.

"What's going on in here? I thought Dani was going to the butterfly house today?"

"I's don't want to go no more." Daniella slowly crawled from the closet, keeping her arms around a squirming bundle wrapped in the blanket.

"What have you got there?" Jane asked, going down on one knee and slowly peeling the blanket back to reveal the large brown eyes of a very young golden retriever puppy. "Oh! She's so precious! Look at those big brown eyes."

The puppy, glad to have its head free from the fabric began to lick everything in sight. Jane's hand. Daniella's face. When it found the lobe of Daniella's ear, it began to chew on it, obviously trying to find some sort of nourishment. The puppy was only a few weeks old by the looks of it. Grace bent down for a closer look and then sighed as she caught the aroma that only came with newborn puppies. *Yep, this little darling still needed its momma.*

"Ouch! Bad Arianna!" Daniella told the puppy, pulling it away from her face and giving it a stern look. "We don't bite. Ever."

The two women exchanged a look and hid their smiles, "Daniella, I think she's trying to find something to eat." Jane ran her hands over the little puppy and then smiled when he immediately tried to suck on her finger. When Dani pulled the puppy tighter into her arms, the puppy's tummy was revealed and Jane bit her lip, already anticipating the argument she knew was coming. "Dani, I think the puppy's hungry. He's not very big and probably still needs his momma." *How did one explain nursing and such to a four-year-old? Ugh!* Grace looked at Jane seeking some sort of help.

"She, Aunt Jane! Didn't you hear me? Her name is Arianna."

"Sweetie, I heard you, but this puppy is a boy." Jane saw the storm cloud form on Dani's young face and hurried to explain, "I don't think he'd like being called by a girl's name, do you?"

Dani looked at the puppy for a moment and then smiled, "Okay, I'll name him Max!"

Grace looked at her daughter and then up at Jane once again. *This is not going to end well!*

Jane quickly caught her silent plea for help and stepped in. "Hey, Dani, why don't you come and show Aunt Jane where you found the puppy?" Jane asked, holding out her hand, smiling when Daniella put her own little one into it. Grace watched her daughter go with Jane, once again thankful for her presence in their house.

Jane was a widower, like Grace, and had come to California right after Christmas to follow her dream of living by the ocean and becoming a chef.

Both of her dreams had come true, in ways no human could have ever orchestrated without a little divine help!

Not only was Jane the new chef, in charge of designing the entire menu for a line of restaurants, but she had finally put her fears of loving aside and followed her heart. She was currently engaged to a FBI agent, Samuel Drackett, and the pair were planning on marrying in a few weeks' time at the beginning of March.

"Aunt Jane, I can keep him, can't I?" Daniella asked, throwing a look at her mother that said 'she'll let me keep the puppy.'

Jane laughed and then told her, "You know better than that, sweetie. Your momma has the final say. And don't you bat those long eyelashes at me – I'm not going to change my mind. Now...can you show me where you found this little guy?"

Daniella started to pout, but then the puppy squirmed and her attention was rerouted. Luckily! Nodding her head, she smiled up at Jane, "I can show you. I went out to get my tennis shoes, 'cause they gots muddy yesterday after it rained, and momma washed them off with the house. I heard him crying by the fence. He was all muddy, but I wiped him all off and he stopped crying."

"Do I want to know what you used to wipe him off with?" Grace asked from behind the duo, closing her eyes as her daughter gave her the answer.

Daniella looked over her shoulder and primly told her, "I used my bath towel from last night. It was still a little wet, but now it's all muddy. It's gonna need a good washin', momma."

Grace nodded as Jane bit her lip to keep from laughing. "Show me where you found the puppy, sugar," Jane asked as they exited into the backyard.

Daniella pointed to a spot by the back fence. Jane and Grace both approached the fence to see a large hole dug beneath it. As they watched, another squirming yellow ball of fur crawled beneath the fence. "Huh? I'm thinking your neighbor has a litter of puppies trying to escape."

Grace nodded, "I'm not even sure who lives there. There used to be an older couple, but after he died, their kids moved her up to Oregon to be closer to them."

Jane scooped up the second puppy, only to hear Daniella behind her, "Goody! Two puppies! Can I keep them both?"

Grace shook her head, "Honey, you can't keep either one of them. We've already discussed how lonely a puppy would be when it had to stay here all day by itself. Besides, these puppies belong to the neighbor and I bet the momma dog is wondering where her babies are."

"Why don't we go knock on the door and see if the neighbor is home?" Jane suggested, crossing her fingers that Daniella would be more interested in seeing the rest of the litter than throwing a morning tantrum.

Daniella looked at the puppies longingly one last time and then slowly nodded, "Do you think the momma dog is really sad her babies crawled away?"

"I'm sure she is. Maybe we can meet the momma dog when we give the babies back," Grace offered, hoping the neighbor was home and hadn't already left for work. She glanced at her watch and cringed. The only way Daniella would get to see the butterfly house was if Grace drove her directly there. *I'll have to call the school and let Mr. Simpson know that's what we're doing. Just as soon as I return these two puppies!*

Chapter 2

Grace, Jane, and a very reluctant four-year-old traipsed across the front yard, walking up to the neighbor's front door and knocking. It was almost 8 o'clock, and Grace hoped they were awake at least. While they waited for someone to answer the door, Grace felt bad for not having come over and introduced herself earlier. *I'm a terrible neighbor! They lived here for months and I don't even know their names!*

A few moments later, a little girl around nine years old opened the front door, but just a crack.

Grace smiled down at her, and asked, "Is your mommy home?" She took in the little girl's appearance, wondering at the sight of her badly tangled blonde hair, dirty pajamas, and large fearful eyes.

The little girl didn't seem inclined to answer, so Grace got down on her level and asked again, "Sweetie, can you go get your mommy for me?"

When the little girl shook her head, Grace became a little concerned. "Is your mommy here?"

The little girl nodded her head, but still didn't answer. "I really need to talk to her." Grace pointed to where Daniella and Jane stood, holding the squirming puppies, "These little guys got under the fence this morning."

The little girl's eyes grew big and she opened the door wider.

"Do these little guys belong to you?" Grace asked softly.

The little girl nodded and then whispered, "Momma's gonna be upset they dug under the fence." She wrung her hands as she finished talking and looked so worried Grace grew even more suspicious.

"What's your name, sweetie?" Grace asked softly, giving her a warm smile of encouragement.

"Emily."

"That's a very pretty name. This is my little girl Daniella, and this is Jane."

"How comes she's not in school, momma?" Daniella asked, peeking around Grace's legs to get a better look at her neighbor.

"Shush!" Grace scolded her before she turned a smile back to Emily and asked once again, "Go get your momma for me."

"I can't. She's too sick to get out of bed this morning. That's why I'm not in school today. She needs my help." Emily stated the fact that her momma was sick as if it were a common occurrence.

Grace and Jane exchanged a concerned look and then Grace asked, "How about you let us help you put these little guys back in the yard and fill in the hole so that your momma doesn't have to do that while she's not feeling well. Would that be okay?"

Emily thought for a moment and then unlatched the screen door, "Okay. But we have to be quiet, momma's got a bad headache this morning."

Grace nodded at her and held the door open for Jane and Daniella to enter. They followed Emily silently through a very well organized living room and out through a sliding door in the dining room.

A large golden retriever greeted them and Jane helped Daniella hold the puppies down so she could sniff her babies. The puppies immediately started crying and squirming to get loose. Daniella put her puppy down and it started rooting around the momma dog's legs.

"They're hungry," Emily said as she picked one of the pups up and carted it over to a large children's swimming pool on the covered porch, depositing it there with its siblings. Jane followed her lead, took the other pup over, and then watched as the momma dog stepped carefully into the pool and lay down. Within seconds, the tiny puppies had settled in and were nursing happily.

"Well, now that we have the puppies taken care of, why don't we see if your momma needs some help?" Grace dusted her hands off and gave Emily another warm smile.

Emily looked doubtful and was about to argue when Jane asked, "Emily, have you had breakfast yet?"

Emily shook her head, looking between the two women as if she was unsure who she should be giving her attention to.

"How about I see if I can round us up some pancakes? I bet your momma has the right ingredients." Jane winked at her, pleased when the little girl smiled tentatively back at her.

"I guess that would be okay. I'm not allowed to use the stove or the oven when she's not around. Usually when mommas this sick I just eat cereal, but then I couldn't get the lid open on the milk this morning."

Grace and Jane exchanged a look and then Jane took over the conversation. "Emily, that's a very good rule your momma has. The oven and the stove can get things really hot, and you could get burned. I tell you what, I'm going to go wash my hands up and see if I can find what I need. Why don't you take Grace in and introduce her to your momma?"

After pausing to consider what was being offered, she finally nodded and led Grace back through the house, to a small bedroom at the back of the house. Grace did her best to look at her surroundings, and was pleased to see that everything was in good repair and the house looked like it had recently been cleaned. Whatever was wrong with Emily's mom was most likely a recent event, or she had some kind of domestic help.

"Momma?" Emily whispered, pushing the door to the room open. Grace followed her inside the small room and looked around. It was a very small room, most likely the smallest one in the house. The only furnishings were a small bedside table and the bed. It looked more like a guest bedroom than a room occupied by someone who lived in the house.

Grace noticed there was very little light in the room, just the sliver that peeked out from under the bathroom door. The curtain over the window was pulled shut to keep the sunlight out.

"Emmy?" a female voice said weakly before ending in a strangled cough.

Emily hurried to the bed where a woman lay, gasping for breath with her eyes closed. Grace followed close behind her and was shocked to see a woman, not much older than she was, but without any hair. None.

Grace took in the rest of the woman's appearance, her heart dropping into her stomach as the past came back to haunt her. *Oh, my! She has cancer!* "Miss...," Grace broke off, not having thought to ask the woman's name.

The woman paused when she heard the strange voice and slowly opened her eyes, "Emmy, who's this?" She made a feeble attempt to sit up in the bed, protecting her child upper most in her mind, but her body was incapable of obeying.

Grace took a step nearer the bed and smiled warmly, "My name is Grace Powers. I live next door to you. Your new arrivals dug a hole beneath the fence between our two houses. I was just returning them when Emily mentioned you weren't feeling very good. I don't mean to pry, but I wondered if there was anything I could do for you."

Victoria tried to push herself up in the bed once more, but her strength just wasn't there. *Stupid drugs!* Grace saw her struggling and hurried to assure her it was unnecessary, "Please, don't wear yourself out."

Jane stuck her head in the door right then, "Hi. I'm Jane from next door." She glanced at the bald woman lying in the bed, and then forced her eyes to look away. Finding Emily's eyes, she directed her comments to the little girl, "I'm about ready to pour the batter into the pan. Do you want to come help me?" Looking back to the woman in the bed, she offered, "I offered to make Emily some pancakes for breakfast. I hope you don't mind, but I searched through the kitchen cupboards."

"No, I don't mind." Emily looked at her mother who slowly nodded her head, "Go on, sweetie. I'll just talk with Grace for a moment."

Emily hugged her mom and then left the room as Jane closed the door. Grace took a breath and then asked, "Cancer?"

Victoria nodded, "Yeah. I had my last chemo session yesterday. I'm in full remission, but they insisted on doing the chemo and radiation as a preventative."

Grace spied a folding chair propped against the wall and retrieved it. Unfolding it, she situated it next to the bed and sat down, "What type of cancer?"

"Breast. They...," Victoria paused, not having had to explain about having her entire left breast removed to anyone but the medical staff. It was an odd conversation to be having, let alone with a virtual stranger.

Grace nodded her head, "I understand. My mom had pancreatic cancer while I was finishing high school. She didn't make it."

"I'm sorry for your loss."

Grace was amazed at the compassion she saw on the sick woman's face. "Thanks. I'm glad you're in remission." The room grew silent for a moment and then Grace asked, "Is Emily your only child?"

Victoria smiled, pride evident on her face as she bragged on her little girl, "Yes. Do you have any children?"

"A little girl who's four. She's in your kitchen right now, most likely trying to figure out a way to convince us both she needs to have her very own puppy."

Victoria's eyes dimmed, "Gosh, I forgot all about the puppies. Could you get Emily for me?"

"Was there something you needed done?" Grace offered. "I could call your husband or..."

"I haven't fed or watered Shelby this morning, and I'll have to find something to stick under the fence. Maybe there's a loose brick... And, there is no husband. Never has been." *Never would be! Not now! No man would want her now!*

"I'm sorry! Uhm...it looked like Emily might have already fed the momma dog, there was plenty of food in her bowl when we put the puppies back. As for the fence, I already filled it in. We'll block it up with something a little stronger this afternoon when the guys stop by."

"Guys?" Victoria asked.

Grace smiled, "Yeah, my boyfriend and Jane's fiancé. Between the two of them, they should be able to puppy proof the fence between our yards."

Victoria closed her eyes as the pain wracking her body and head became too much to push away.

Grace watched as her skin took on a grey tinge and the skin around her mouth and eyes grew tight. *She's in so much pain!* "Victoria, do you have something you can take?"

"I can't," she gasped, fighting to push the pain away as she'd done so many days in the past. "Not with Emily at home. Usually I take her to school and then if I need something, I have a few hours for it to wear off. I knew I couldn't drive her today, so she's missing – again. She's missed so many days of school this year..."

Grace watched the weary woman, remembering how sick the chemo had made her own mom. The cancer had been bad; but the chemicals used to treat it had been even worse. Causing mind-wrenching body aches, joint swelling, and overwhelming nausea. All combined together they were horrid. And then came the massive headaches. Worse than any migraine, and almost untreatable without completely being knocked unconscious.

She watched Victoria and knew instantly she was near her breaking point. She needed to take something to make the pain go away while her body absorbed the load of chemicals it had received yesterday.

"Victoria, I know you don't know me, but I would be happy to run Emily to school for you. That way you could take your pain meds and get some relief before this afternoon." She could see the woman about to refuse and then softly laid a hand upon her arm, "Please. We both know you need to rest. And Emily's pretty worried about you. Who's going to care for her if you get so ill they have to put you in the hospital?"

"She sleeps in the room with me. We've already been down that road when I had my surgery. I'm a registered nurse. Before I got sick, I worked on the oncology ward, treating women just like myself. I never in a million years thought I'd be on the receiving end. When I had my surgery, several friends tried to get Emily to leave the hospital with them, but she adamantly refused to go. My coworkers did what they could – setting up a cot in the employee lounge, but Emily refused to leave my side, so they set up a cot in the room for her to use."

"What about school?" Grace asked.

"She goes when I can take her. The bus doesn't come here because we're too close to the school, but I can't let a nine-year-old walk two miles each way!"

"She seems very intelligent," Grace offered, wondering which school the young girl attended. Simpson Preparatory Academy, along with three public schools, was within the two-mile distance Victoria had mentioned. *It would be great if she went to the same school as Dani.*

"She is. They were talking about trying to move her ahead in her studies, but now, she'll be lucky if she can move to the next grade." Tears filled Victoria's eyes as the impact her illness was having on her daughter was once again revealed. "I hate this!"

Grace was close to tears as well. Having done the single mother thing and just come through a horrible scare with her own daughter, she could understand where Victoria's emotion was coming from. Her heart had stopped when there had been a possibility that Daniella might have leukemia. When the tests had come back negative, she'd been so relieved and thankful, she would never forget that moment. It was as if her life had been given back to her.

"I don't have time right now, but I would love to spend more time talking to you. Why don't I take Emily to school today, and pick her up this afternoon as well? That will give you a chance to let the chemicals wear off."

Victoria looked at the woman sitting beside her bed and decided she must be some sort of angel sent to save her and her daughter. She was so used to doing everything on her own; she didn't have any idea of how to accept the kind offer without breaking down in tears. *You don't have to do this on your own today!*

Unable to keep the emotion at bay, she let the tears fall from her eyes and nodded. "Thank you. I know I shouldn't do this, but something tells me I can trust you."

Grace nodded her head, laying a gentle hand upon her arm, "You can. I'll watch over Emily as if she were my own. I promise."

Victoria nodded. "I believe you."

"Which school does Emily attend?" Grace asked, already trying to calculate how late Daniella was going to be now.

"Simpson Preparatory Academy. At least for right now. They said they would do what they could to help with her missing so many days, but I..."

"Hey, you're in luck. Daniella just started pre-school there this term. I can take Emily to school today and I'll let her teacher know what's going on."

Once again, Victoria was brought to tears by the generosity of the woman from next door. *Thank you!* "I don't even know what to say, but 'Thanks.'"

Grace smiled at her, "No thanks needed. Tell me where your pain pills are."

"In the bathroom, top shelf. I didn't want Emily to...," her voice died off as a horrible cough consumed her.

Grace entered the bathroom, finding the bottle of pills, and then filling a disposable cup with water. Returning to the bed, she asked, "One pill or two?"

"Two, please. The first few days are always the worst." Victoria took the pills and the cup of water, grateful when Grace gently lifted her head up from the pillow so she could swallow the pills.

"I remember. My older sister did the majority of the care for my mom, insisting I finish school, but I still remember how bad it could get. Do you need me to put a waste basket next to the bed?" Grace remembered the nausea that would plague her mom the first few days after a chemo round. *As if losing your hair and being wracked with pain wasn't enough to go through!*

"No, I finished all of that yesterday." Victoria handed back the empty cup and tried to keep her eyes open. *She was so tired!*

"Good." Grace returned the pill bottle to the bathroom cabinet, wetting a clean washrag and bringing it back. She gently wiped Victoria's forehead, returning her smile with one of her own. One done, she folded the chair up and put it back against the wall and then pulled the walker that had been leaning next to it over and opened it up.

"Please do yourself a favor and use this if you need to. I'm going to grab the girls and get them to school. I'll have Jane stop by and say 'Hello' for a minute before she heads to work. When I come back this afternoon, be prepared to tell us how we can help you out until you have your feet back under you. And before you politely decline my offer, please know that I can be tenacious when I want to be. Neighbors help each other. End of story."

Grace didn't wait for the shocked woman to reply; she smiled at her and then left the bedroom, shutting the door behind her. Well, this had certainly added another element to her life, but added it had been. Grace had never shied away from a challenge, or offering help when it was needed, and she wasn't about to start now. Daniella was going to see what it meant to "Love your neighbor" in living color.

Chapter 3

Grace arrived at the school with both girls; Emily having dressed herself in the required school uniform of plaid skirt and polo shirt. Jane had worked her magic on her tangled hair, and she now sported two identical braids, tied with matching ribbons on the ends.

The pre-school classes had already left for the butterfly house, but the school secretary offered to call Mr. Simpson and let him know that Grace would be bringing Daniella over shortly. While Grace went to talk with Emily's teacher, Daniella stayed with the secretary and watched the fish in the large saltwater tank that greeted the children each morning.

Grace explained what was happening with Emily's mom, and the teacher promised to compile of list of homework the child needed to work on to catch up with the rest of the class. Grace and Jane would both pitch in and see that she finished the school year with the rest of her classmates.

After dropping Daniella off at the butterfly house, she ran a few errands. She then went grocery shopping for both households, arriving back at the school just in time to pick up both little girls.

"Dani, how was the butterfly house?" Grace asked as she pulled away from the school.

"Momma, we gots to see a canterpull morphisize."

Grace laughed when she saw Emily's expression of confusion. Interpreting, she asked Dani, "Do you mean you got to see a caterpillar metamorphosis?"

"That's what I said!" Dani told her.

"No you didn't. You said..."

Grace saw the look on her daughter's face and hurried to interrupt the tantrum she could see was forthcoming, "So Emily, did you have a good day at school?"

"Yes. My teacher gave me a big envelope to give to momma, and made me bring my books home."

"That's good, honey. I talked with your teacher and Jane and I are going to help you get caught up on your school work. Your momma's pretty worried about that."

"Oh."

"So, tell me what needs to be done when you get home."

"Well, I need to play with Shelby and give her some time away from the puppies. Momma says it helps her tolerate them better. But usually she just gets on my bed and sleeps. She never wants to play anymore."

Grace laughed, "She will. She's just tired right now. Pretty soon the puppies will be old enough to eat puppy food, and she won't be so tired all the time. How many puppies are there?"

"Nine."

"Nine! I want one!" Daniella informed her mother.

"We've already talked about this, Dani."

"The puppies can't go to new homes for two more weeks. Momma said they have to be at least eight weeks old. She was talking about starting to wean them this week…"

"What's wean?" Daniella asked Emily, curiosity written all over her face at the new word.

"It means they won't nurse anymore, and they'll eat puppy food."

"What do they eat now?" Daniella asked, and Grace cringed as she struggled to figure out a way to explain. She didn't have to as Emily gladly took over the task of explaining how the puppies currently ate.

Daniella listened attentively and Grace knew there would be questions asked later when it was just she and her daughter. For now, her curiosity had been assuaged and she turned her thoughts to other things.

Michael was waiting in the driveway when they arrived home, and she smiled at him as she put the car into park and got out. "Hey, I didn't expect to see you for another couple of hours."

Michael gave her a brief kiss on the cheek, and then opened the back door and helped Dani unbuckle her car seat. "Hey, Princess. How was the butterfly house?"

"Awesome! I saws a canterpull…"

"Caterpillar, silly," Emily corrected her with a shake of her head.

Michael looked at the newcomer and then back at Grace. "New friend?"

"New neighbor. Emily, this is Dr. Michael Simpson. Michael, this is Emily from next door."

"Hey, we have a Mr. Simpson at my school," Emily offered with a smile.

"He's my brother."

"Really? That's cool. Hey Dani, wanna go see the puppies?" Emily asked, already dragging her heavy backpack across the lawn.

Daniella looked at Grace and when she nodded, she took off running after the older girl. Michael watched her leave, and then turned and looked at Grace, "Somehow, I feel like I've missed something."

"I'll explain everything while you help me unload the groceries," Grace promised with a smile.

"I can do that."

Michael and Grace made short work of unloading the groceries and storing them away. When the only bags left were the ones that belonged next door, she picked two of them up, gesturing for Michael to grab the rest, "Come with me. Dani's probably already worn out her welcome with Shelby."

They entered the backyard through the side gate, hearing the chatter of little girls as they rounded the house. Daniella sat in the middle of the backyard with Emily, surrounded by nine little bundles of fur. Shelby had climbed back into the kiddy pool for a much needed nap.

Michael took in the scene and then nodded towards the adult dog, "Shelby, I presume?"

"Yeah. Poor thing. She's resorted to sleeping in the pool to get some rest."

"Momma, I don't want one puppy now," Daniella informed her as she drew closer.

"You don't?" Grace asked in surprise.

"She wants to keep them all. She said you wouldn't let her have a puppy because it would get lonely all by itself."

Michael laughed as he whispered, "Now I can't wait to see how you get out of this one!"

"Oh, shush! You're no help! Daniella, whatever you and Emily have cooked up, it isn't going to happen."

"But momma!"

"Don't go there, Dani."

"But, Miss Grace, she only wants to keep three puppies! Not all of them!"

"Emily, thank you for clarifying that." *Not!* "Have you checked on your momma yet?"

Emily nodded, "She's sleeping really sound and I didn't want to wake her up. I checked to make sure she's still breathing and everything..."

Michael was horrified upon hearing the little girl's words, and turned and headed for the open patio door. When Grace immediately followed him, he waited for a space of a heartbeat before he demanded, "Explain. Please."

Grace saw the concern on his face and hurried to fill him in. "Emily's mom, Victoria, is just finishing up chemo for breast cancer. She had her last chemo session yesterday and it made her really sick."

"Why isn't the woman in the hospital?" he asked, trying to keep his voice down.

"Because she has no one else to look after Emily. She's in full remission, and she told me she usually does well enough to handle things, but this last dose looks like it really did a number on her."

"Where is she?" Michael asked, switching into doctor mode that fast.

"Michael, she's in the back bedroom, but I should warn you – she's a registered nurse who worked on the oncology floor prior to getting sick. She's not being careless or neglectful, okay?"

Michael closed his eyes and then nodded his head. "Sorry. Have I told you how much I detest cancer?"

"The fact that you've dedicated your life to treating that very disease was kind of a big hint," she told him, hugging him close. Stepping away from him a moment later, she headed down the hallway, "I need to check on her for myself."

Michael followed her to the door and then whispered, "Why don't you go in and see if she's awake? I don't want to make her uncomfortable, but if she's still sick, please let her know I'm here and would be happy to see if I can make her more comfortable."

Grace leaned up and kissed his cheek, "Thank you. I'll just be a minute."

Grace entered the room, noticing that the walker had been folded back up and placed against the wall. Shaking her head at the stubbornness of the woman in the bed, she quietly whispered her name, "Victoria?"

The woman's eyes fluttered and then opened, "Grace? Where's Emily?" she asked as she looked around the room for her daughter.

"She and Dani are in the backyard playing with the puppies. Shelby is sleeping inside the kiddie pool."

Victoria smiled, "That poor dog. The only time she really gets to sleep is when the puppies can't get to her. Normally, we let her inside for a few hours during the day, otherwise the puppies want to nurse all day long."

"That's what Emily was telling me. She also said that they're ready to start weaning."

Victoria sighed and then shakily tried to push herself up on the pillows. Grace saw her struggle and hurried to help her. "Thanks," she offered once she was settled.

"The puppies do need to start weaning, but I guess it will have to wait for a few more days. I'm just not up to it right now."

"A few more days won't hurt anything. Are you feeling any better?"

"I was, but my headache is back again." Victoria swallowed and closed her eyes wearily.

"Why don't I get you another pain pill?" Grace offered.

"No. I..."

"Look, I know you're hurting. My boyfriend helped me bring some groceries over and is right outside the door. He's a doctor and if it's okay with you, he offered to see if he could do anything to help ease your pain."

Victoria smiled, "He's welcome to try. Frankly, I'm glad this was the last chemo session. If they'd all been this bad, I don't know if I would have been able to stick it out and finish them."

"I'm glad it was your last one. Let me get Michael."

Grace opened the door and gestured Michael inside. Turning she made the introductions, "Michael, meet Victoria Drake. Victoria, Dr. Michael Simpson."

Victoria looked at the man standing next to her bed and then back at Grace, "You didn't tell me your boyfriend was Dr. Simpson."

"Does it make a difference?" Grace asked, seeing the look on the woman's face.

"No, but...I'm sorry. Dr. Simpson, it's nice to finally meet you."

Michael had listened to the exchange with a bemused expression on his face, "Have we met before?"

"No, but we used some of your treatment protocols in the oncology unit where I worked. You may have developed them for use with kids, but they work with adults as well."

"That's good to know. Grace here tells me you're in remission, and just finished your last chemo session."

"Yesterday. This one's been pretty rough," she informed him. Grace listened as she proceeded to give him a rundown of her medical condition and symptoms, most of which just sounded like a bunch of big words to Grace.

Michael, on the other hand, listened and asked more questions before he went to look at the medication she had available. He returned a few minutes later with several pills in his hand and a cup of water. Handing them to her, he explained what the pills were and Grace was relieved when Victoria took them without arguing.

"They won't make you too sleepy to still watch over Emily, but should help with the pain and the headache."

"Thank you. I don't know why I didn't think of that combination myself."

"Hey, I'm happy I was around to help. Now, I'll let you two ladies talk for a bit while I go meet some puppies. I'll do my best to dissuade the girls from their current plans."

Grace rolled her eyes. Victoria stared at the closing door and then asked, "Do I want to know what our daughters are cooking up?"

Grace smiled, "Well, let's see. I told Daniella several weeks ago we couldn't have a puppy because it wouldn't be fair to leave it at home every day, all by itself. Emily pointed out that you have nine puppies. Between them, they have decided that if Dani keeps three of them, the puppies won't be lonely, and they will both have a puppy to play with, plus an extra one."

"Oh, no! Emily knows we can't keep the puppies. Why would she suggest Dani keep three of them?" Victoria looked so worried; Grace couldn't help but smile.

"Believe me, I'm sure the idea originated with my precocious four-year-old. Her mind works faster than a speeding bullet. It's all I can do most days to try to keep up with her."

Victoria giggled, "I remember when Emily was that age. Don't worry, pretty soon you figure them out and then they change their tactics."

"Great! Thanks for that pep talk!" Grace made a face at the woman and then laughed. "Now, I told you to think about what you needed help with. Start talking."

Grace spent the next thirty minutes working out a schedule to help Victoria manage both Emily and the puppies, and to help Emily catch up with her schoolwork. Victoria tried to argue that Grace was taking on too much, but finally gave up when Grace threatened to have Jane come talk to her. Evidently Jane had made sure Victoria knew she was going to be getting help and she might as well just give in and save her energy since arguing was going to get her nowhere.

"I don't even know what to say. I mean, I don't know anything about you," Victoria said, close to tears once again.

"Victoria..."

"Tori. My friends call me Tori."

"Tori, I'm glad we can help you out. Now, I picked up some food from the deli. How about I show Emily where everything is and get her started on some schoolwork before I leave? I've written my home, and both Jane and my cell phone numbers down on a card and left it by the phone in the kitchen.

"If you need anything, or Emily needs anything, I want you to call me. I don't care what time of day it is." Grace waited until Victoria nodded her head and then smiled, "Great. I'll come over around 7:15 to make sure Emily's getting ready for school. Have a good night."

Grace called Emily into the house and showed her what she'd picked up for dinner and then got her started on some makeup spelling worksheets. She set the little girl's alarm clock for 6:45 a.m. and promised to arrive early enough to help her with her hair.

Michael and Dani had headed back to the house, with Michael promising to have a tea party with her before dinnertime. Grace left by the side gate, smiling as she watched Shelby with her puppies. Motherhood took many forms, and watching the mother dog with her nine puppies, and then thinking about the early days when all she'd had was one Dani to care for, she was very glad that humans rarely had more than one child at a time.

Chapter 4

*C*astle Peaks, Montana ...

"So, Jackson, what do you think of our plans so far?" Sara asked the young man sitting across from her. The Mercer-Brownell Foundation was all set up and ready to go – on paper. All they were waiting on now was for the ground to unfreeze so construction could begin. Well, that and for the proper staff to be located.

She and Trent had been back in Montana for only a few days when the resumes had started pouring in. She'd placed the ad on two internet sites that catered to medical professionals before rushing to California to be with her sister and niece while they checked her niece for leukemia. Thankfully, the tests had come back negative, and she and Trent had flown back home to take care of their own responsibilities.

Sara had never imagined there would be so many people who wanted to move to Montana. Especially some so well qualified. That's where Jackson Myers came in.

As a board certified cancer specialist, he had also trained extensively with several naturopathic and holistic medicine practitioners in ways to minimize pain, slow cancer growth, and heal the whole body. He was young, not afraid to think out of the box, and had jumped at the chance to interview for the position of Lead Physician.

"I have to tell you, Sara," Jackson said, shaking his head at how unbelievably lucky he felt to be given this interview, "I would love to work here. And that probably doesn't adequately express how excited I am about this project. It's everything I've ever wanted to do, all in one place."

Sara smiled at his enthusiasm and then asked, "So tell me a little bit about Jackson Myers. Not the stuff on your resume, but about you. I'd like to know more about the man who's going to be heading up the medical side of things. Where did you grow up? Siblings? Girlfriends? Hobbies?"

Jackson looked at her with his mouth open and then shook his head and asked, "Really? I thought..."

Sara nodded, "The job is yours if you want it. But we're a tight knit little group up here, and I'd like to get a feel for who you are as a person."

"That's it? You get to make the decision all by yourself?" Jackson asked, impressed but also cautious.

"Bill trusts my judgment. You are exactly what I've been looking for."

Jackson grinned and then settled back in his seat. "I accept. Just in case after I tell you about myself, you decide to take the offer back. I accept the position."

Sara laughed with him and then waved her hand for him to get on with the storytelling.

"Well, let's see. I grew up in a small town on the Oregon coast. There were only a few thousand people in the town, so I understand how tightly intertwined lives can get. Anyway, I played basketball all through high school, and dated the head cheerleader." Jackson broke off as sad memories filled his head. He'd dated the head cheerleader and they'd been planning to get married right after graduation. Just before the start of the fourth quarter, she had moved. No notice. No messages. Her mother had loaded up her and her younger sister, leaving in the middle of the night and no one had ever heard from them again.

He'd been heartbroken, and that event had forever changed his life. He'd never forgotten his first girlfriend. His first love! He'd spent the entire summer after graduation trying to track her down, but it was as if she'd never existed.

Her mother had arranged for her mail to be forwarded, and the house they had been renting sat vacant until the landlord finally had their belongings hauled off. His parents had been supportive, his dad had even hired a private investigator to try to determine what had happened to them, but each lead had turned up empty.

It wasn't until the end of that horrible summer, when the reality of his relationship with his girlfriend had surfaced. Jackson had gone to the next town over with some friends and they had run into a group of basketball players from a rival school.

When several of the young men had made disparaging comments about his missing girlfriend, Jackson had seen red and thrown the first punch. A huge fight had ensued, resulting in all of the boys spending the night in the local jail. No charges had been filed and they had all been released the next morning.

The boys had taken great pleasure in telling Jackson how his girlfriend had been secretly dating the star player of their team, and how they had seen her making out with him on more than one occasion. Jackson had ben furious. He and Michelle had agreed to save themselves for marriage, and while they had shared a few kisses here and there, he had always respected her decision.

When his own teammates had reluctantly admitted they'd suspected she was cheating on him, he'd felt his entire world tip on its axis. He'd loved Michelle and thought she'd felt the same way about him. He'd been duped, and since that time, had been very hesitant to give his trust, in any type of relationship. Friend or romantic.

Bringing himself back to the present, he looked up and saw Sara watching him, "Those thoughts didn't seem very pleasant."

"They weren't. Sorry about that. My senior year of high school didn't quite end the way I would have wanted it to. My girlfriend disappeared one night with her mother and sister; I never saw or heard from her again. It was probably the darkest time in my life." *She doesn't need to know the rest. What point would it serve?*

Sara was thoughtful before she asked, "You've never gotten married?"

"No. I left for college at the end of that summer and then there was med school, and internships..."

Sara smiled at him gently, "You can stop. I get it. I hope that one day you find what you need to complete you. But until then, I can't wait for you to set up shop here. The construction should be completed by the end of the summer, but I'd love for you to move up here before then.

"I'd love to have a professional eye on things as the facility is put together. I know what I like from an aesthetic perspective, but I'm afraid I have no idea of what might be needed from the medical side of things."

Jackson nodded and then said, "I could probably be back up here whenever you think is good. I've already given my two weeks' notice at my previous work, so I only have to pack up my stuff."

"That sounds really good. Could you be here by the first of March?" Sara looked at his resume, not remembering exactly where he was currently living. When she saw San Diego, she smiled at him, "You live in San Diego?"

Jackson nodded, "Yes. Well, a suburb outside San Diego. I've been there for the last eighteen months learning more about Chinese holistic medicine, acupuncture, herbal remedies..."

"Acupressure?" Sara asked, wondering just how far his training had gone.

"Why, yes. Although, I've never had an opportunity to use that particular treatment on a patient."

"Well, you should. In fact, that's actually how this foundation came together." Sara proceeded to give him the condensed version of helping her mother and then Miriam Mercer. Jackson listened attentively for all of two minutes and then he took a piece of paper and started to take notes.

"That is very interesting. I would love to watch your technique..."

"Oh, but I'm not trained or anything. That's why I need someone like you to make sure everything's being done correctly."

"Sara, the first thing I learned about natural medicine is listen to yourself. It sounds like you did a fine job of helping both your mother and Mrs. Mercer; don't ever lose sight of that. Sometimes all of the medical knowledge in the world doesn't do one bit of good for the patient."

Sara listened to his passionate speech and then nodded her head in acceptance. "Thank you for that."

"You bet. Now to answer your question..."

Sara waved his answer off, "You know what? Forget it. I'll get to know you just like you'll get to know all of us. One day at a time." She stood up and held out her hand, pleased when Jackson followed her lead and did the same.

"Welcome aboard. Now, I believe Bill is planning a little get together for dinner this evening. If you don't mind tagging along while I run a few errands before I pick up my husband, you're welcome to ride with us."

Jackson smiled and nodded. "That sounds good. Maybe you can answer some questions about the town..."

Sara started shaking her head, "No. Not me. I arrived here a week before Christmas. Now Trent, my husband, he can probably answer any question you have. As for me, I still feel like a visitor most of the time."

Jackson, looking shocked, replied, "You moved here just before Christmas?"

Sara grabbed her purse and headed for the door. "Come along. I fill you in on the way."

Chapter 5

San Diego, California, later that same day...

S "Samuel?" Jane called, having arrived at his beachfront home, and already played fetch with Lucky down on the beach for ten minutes.

"In here," called the voice she was quickly coming to love the sound of. She wandered through the house to find Samuel standing on a ladder, replacing a burned out light bulb in his office.

She waited until he was finished before speaking. "I see you're hard at work."

"Always. How was your day?" Samuel asked, climbing down from the ladder and giving her a brief kiss.

"Great! The chefs I selected are fabulous. We all seem to get along really well for only having worked together for a week now."

"Why are you so surprised? You're one of the easiest people I know to get along with," Samuel told her, taking her hand and leading her back into the living area. He opened the screen door, letting Lucky inside and laughing when the dog promptly lay down at his feet.

He dutifully bent over and scratched the offered tummy, saying, "You are spoiled rotten!" Rising back to his feet, he was surprised to see a look of doubt on Jane's face. "What's wrong?"

"Well... I've been thinking... I don't know that many people here yet." She obviously had something on her mind, so Samuel was quiet and just let her say what she wanted to say – in her own timing. "I don't want to get married here!"

Jane cringed as she heard the words leave her mouth and saw the stunned look on Samuel's face. She hurried to make sure he didn't misunderstand her, "It's not that I don't want to still get married, I just don't want to get married in California."

Samuel had thought his heart would crumble when he'd first heard her say she didn't want to get married. But as her words registered, he kicked himself for not having thought about her feelings earlier. "No problem. I can marry you anywhere. California. Castle Peaks. Shoot, if you want to fly to Timbuktu and get married, I'll do what I can to make it happen."

"Timbuktu? Really?" Jane asked with a hopeful tone to her voice as she teased him.

"Well, maybe not Timbuktu. I don't know if you can even get married there, but if you want to go home to Castle..."

Jane shook her head with a smile, "Home is here now. But all of the people I would want to be at my wedding are in Montana. Well, except for you and Grace and Dani."

Samuel pulled her into this chest and rested his chin on her head, "Jane, if you want to get married in Castle Peaks, then that's what we'll do. But make it soon, okay?"

"Afraid I might find someone else?" Jane teased.

"Well, I saw you looking at the gorillas the last time we went to the zoo. That guy with the silver hair going down his back seemed to have caught your eye."

Jane laughed and pushed away from him, "Don't you know it. Dani and I have a thing for the apes. Which reminds me, we had quite the excitement while you were up in Los Angeles. Grace's neighbor has a litter of the cutest puppies."

"Wow! Her neighbor is a dog?" Samuel teased her.

"No! Her neighbor has a dog with nine of the cutest puppies I've ever seen."

"Nine?! Wow! That's a lot of puppies. What breed are they?" Samuel pulled the steaks he had been marinating in the fridge out and began preparing them for the grill.

"Golden retrievers. Just like Lucky. Anyway, they managed to dig their way under the fence and Dani found one of them. Before Grace or I knew it, she had brought the puppy into the house, named it Arianna, and was hiding it in her closet."

"She didn't? That little minx. How long was the puppy in there before you all found it?"

"Only a few minutes. Dani wouldn't leave it alone. She had this little tent made inside her closet, and was willing to forego the butterfly house to keep it hidden. Unfortunately, it wasn't a girl puppy and she had to change the name to Max."

"Max, huh? So Grace is letting her keep it?" Samuel questioned.

Jane laughed, "No. The puppies aren't fully weaned yet, but I will be very surprised if Dani doesn't end up with at least one of them. The neighbor also has a nine-year-old little girl named Emily, who seems to have taken a liking to Dani."

"Does she like to play dress up and have tea parties?" Samuel asked hopefully. Daniella had been trying for weeks to convince him to play dress up with her, but each time, Samuel had managed to elude her plastic earrings and tiaras.

"You are going to have to give in one of these days and play with her. She'll think you don't like her if you don't." Jane scolded him, taking the potatoes from the oven and preparing to scrape the insides out.

"Yeah, well I think Michael has everything well under control for us both. I'll just leave the wearing of the jewelry to him." Samuel headed towards the grill, not waiting for Jane to reply back.

Jane shook her head and then scraped the potatoes into a bowl. She added sour cream, bacon, cheese, garlic powder, salt and pepper and then mixed it all up. Once she was satisfied that it was seasoned to her liking, she spooned the mixture back into the potato shells and popped them back into the oven.

Since Samuel hadn't come back inside, she wandered out onto the deck to find him almost to the beach where Lucky danced around with her stick. *That dog never tires of the game!* When he looked back up at the house, she waved at him and then watched him throw the stick down the beach half a dozen times.

She checked the steaks, turning them twice before he rejoined her on the deck. He was rubbing his shoulder and she smiled at him, "Arm sore?"

"Yeah. I need to find her a smaller stick; one that doesn't weigh as much." Currently, Lucky's stick was almost three-feet long, all the bark had been removed, and it was worn smooth from being handled so much.

"Why don't you just throw a ball for her?" Jane asked, thinking about the tennis balls she used to throw for the family dog when she was a little girl.

"Because she eats them."

Jane looked at him with a look of disbelief on her face. "Really? Like, chews them up and ingests them?"

"Yeah, sometimes. She bites on them until she punctures them with her teeth. Once that happens, the ball doesn't even last a day before I find it lying in pieces all over the house. Most of the time, she loses interest in them after they fall apart, but there have been a couple of times where I only found half of the ball. I have to assume she ate the rest of it."

Lucky chose that moment to come up onto the deck, stick in mouth, and tail beating a rhythm on the side of the deck. Jane scratched behind the dog's ears, "Silly mutt. You're supposed to chase the ball, not eat it."

The timer on the oven went off and Jane hurried to remove the potatoes from the oven, while Samuel brought their steak in from the grill. They ate and discussed the other aspects of their day, before the conversation turned back to their upcoming wedding.

"I guess I should probably call Trent and make sure he doesn't mind us having the wedding in Castle Peaks."

"You know both he and Sara are going to be thrilled to host the wedding. In fact, why don't you give them a call right now? Otherwise, you'll worry about it all night."

Jane blushed, knowing that Samuel was right, "Okay. But he's going to want to know when we want to have it."

"Well, grab a calendar and let's figure this out. It shouldn't be too hard. Grace and Daniella will want to come so it probably needs to be during their two-weeks off in March. Julian and Trevor's trials aren't set till later in April, so I can take some time off whenever we want during the month of March."

After spending several minutes looking at the calendar, they settled on March fifteenth, provided Castle Peaks could accommodate their wedding that week. Samuel could already see the worry beginning, and grabbed the phone, dialing Trent before Jane could protest.

"Hello?"

"Trent, Samuel."

"Hey, how's California?"

"Warm and sunny. Wish you were here?" Samuel asked, having played this game with Trent often over the years.

"Now why would I want to give up shoveling snow for hours upon hours, just to have to apply sunscreen to my lily white body and lie in the sun all day?"

"I saw you all were going to get some more snow up there."

"You would have heard correctly. We got ten inches last night, and it's been snowing all day. The only people still happy about the snow are the skiers and ski resort owners. I, and the rest of Montana, are ready for spring about now."

Samuel chuckled before saying, "I'm going to put you on speaker phone so Jane and I can both talk and hear." Samuel looked at her with a no after pushing the right button.

"Trent?"

"Jane, how's the new kitchen working out?"

"Trent, it's so cool. And I would love to tell you all about it, but that's not why we're calling. Samuel and I have been talking, and I really don't want to get married here in California where I don't know very many people. I was wondering if you thought it would be possible for us to come to Castle Peaks for the ceremony."

"Really? You want to get married here? That sounds fantastic. Sara will be excited when she hears that."

"Is she there?" Jane asked.

"Not right now. She's meeting with Bill and the new medical director of the foundation tonight."

"She hired someone?" Samuel asked. "That was quick."

"I agree, but once you meet this young man, you'll understand how she made her decision so quickly. When were you guys wanting to have the ceremony?"

"March fifteenth. Grace and Daniella will be able to travel that week without missing work or school."

"That sounds good. Why don't I talk to Pastor Jameson in the morning and make sure that date works for him? I can let you know what he says and you all can make your plans from there."

"Thanks Trent."

"Don't thank me, Jane. This is as much your home as it is mine. You know mom and dad probably won't be home by then, right?"

"Yeah, but I don't want to wait until the fall. They'll understand why I didn't wait."

"Yes, they will. Okay, I'll talk to everyone and then have Sara call you tomorrow. She can coordinate whatever you need on this end."

"Great! Talk to you tomorrow!" Jane pushed the button to end the call, smiling in happiness as she looked at Samuel.

"Now that's what I like to see," he commented, using a finger to trace her smiling lips. "You happy!"

"You make me happy." Jane nipped his finger playfully and then collapsed back against the couch cushions. "If you had asked me three months ago if I could ever see myself this happy again, I would have said 'No' and laughed at you."

"I would have been right there with you. It's amazing how quickly things can change."

"That it is. Would you change anything, if you could?" Samuel asked, watching Jane's eyes.

"No. Would you?" Jane asked, looking right back at him.

"Yes, the amount of time it took for us to get to this place. I feel like we wasted a bunch of years, being unhappy, when all we needed to do was to take a step out of our comfort zones and have a little faith."

Jane considered his statement and then shook her head, "It wouldn't have been the same. Three years ago. Five years ago. Even one year ago, we weren't the same people."

"Probably not. This is one of those instances where you're not supposed to analyze things too much, isn't it?"

Jane smiled up at him and then kissed him tenderly on the lips, "Yes. It doesn't really matter how long it took us to get here, the important thing is that we arrived."

"Good point! Now, how about we take a walk along the beach before you head home?"

"That sounds really nice. I missed you the last few days. How did things go up in court?"

Samuel led her down the deck stairs to the beach and then tossed Lucky's stick down the beach. "Good. We managed to get a different judge assigned to the case and it looks like Trevor and Julian will be spending quite a bit of time in solitary confinement while they await their trials."

"That's got to set your mind at ease somewhat," she said, watching Lucky come running back with the stick.

"Yeah! With that out of the way, I can focus on finally making you my wife." They walked down the beach a little further before they turned and headed back. After walking her to her car, Samuel kissed her tenderly, murmuring in her ear, "Drive safely. I love you."

"I love you too. I can't wait to marry you," Jane told him, finding it harder than ever to leave him at the end of the day. Only a few more weeks and then they would be married, starting their lives together and making new memories.

Chapter 6

C*astle Peaks, Montana ...*

"Sara, I have to say, I really like that young man," Bill Mercer told her as they stood next to the fireplace in his living room. Bill Mercer had insisted on hosting a special dinner to give some of the townsfolk a chance to meet Jackson. It had been a nice chance for everyone to get better acquainted in an informal setting, and Sara was in agreement – Jackson Myers was the perfect man to head up the Mercer-Brownell Foundation's medical team.

"His credentials are amazing for someone who's only twenty-seven." Sara felt so lucky to have found someone like Jackson, and she just knew that his coming to Castle Peaks was meant to be.

"When is he planning to move up here?" Bill asked, having discussed everything else with the young man but that.

"First part of March is what we discussed earlier today. He's already finished his work back in California, and can pack up and move anytime. With the wedding happening March 15th, I didn't want him arriving only a few days before and everyone being busy doing other things."

Sara had arrived home several nights earlier to the news that Samuel and Jane wanted to get married in Castle Peaks. Pastor Jameson had readily agreed to perform the ceremony, and the date had been locked down. Grace and Daniella would be flying in on the 12th, and Samuel and Jane would be arriving a few days prior to that.

"The first part of March should be fine," Bill nodded his head. "I'm glad Jane's coming home so we can all see her get married. That girl has had a tough life and deserves her own little slice of happiness."

"I couldn't agree with you more," Sara said. She watched Jackson laugh at something Dr. Baker said, and then turned to Bill, "He'll need to find someplace to live, but I was hoping you or Trent might be able to direct him there. Being so new to town myself, I really haven't a clue where to even begin."

Trent overheard his wife's comment as he came up behind her and wrapped his arms around her waist, "Who needs a place to live?"

"Jackson does. He's planning to move up here the first of March."

Trent thought for a moment and then nodded his head, "Well, there's the Beckett place. It's been sitting empty for almost a year, and the place is rather large for one person, but I think it's the only vacant property around."

Bill nodded his head, "That sounds about right. Jim Beckett passed away right before Easter last year," he told Sara, "His four of kids came from across the country for the funeral, but not one of them wants to move back to Castle Peaks. I'll give Dillon a call tomorrow and see if he and his siblings are interested in selling the place."

Pastor Jameson nodded in agreement, "I can't see why he wouldn't want to. Let me know if he pushes back any. I might have to give him a friendly reminder of the fact that the community has been taking care of the yard and the weeds this last year without any sort of compensation."

Sara looked at her husband and smiled. "That's what's so nice about living in a small town. In California, it was hard to get your neighbors to even say a kind word, let alone help with yard work."

Bill patted her shoulder. "We take care of each other around here."

"I can see that." Sara looked over and noticed Jackson hide a yawn behind his hand. "It looks like our guest of honor is ready to turn in."

Everyone looked in that direction and then Trent suggested they start heading home themselves. They could drop Jackson off at the B&B on their way.

Sara's cell phone rang just as she made a move to follow Trent and she turned towards the other end of the room for some privacy as she answered the phone, "Hello?"

"Hey, sis. How's it going up there?"

"Gracie! Hey, it's really good to hear from you. Things are going fantastic. In fact, I hired a medical director for the foundation the other day. A young man who just happens to live outside San Diego."

"Wow! The world's getting smaller and smaller."

Sara chuckled, "Isn't it though?"

"Yeah, hey. The reason I called was I wanted to ask you a question about the acupressure techniques you used on mom. I've been struggling to remember, but I haven't been able to come up with anything yet."

Sara stopped moving and held still as she asked, "Gracie, who's hurting?"

Grace heard the fear in her sister's voice and hurried to explain, "It's not anyone you know. I met my next door neighbor earlier this week and she's recovering from breast cancer chemo. From what I could tell, she's suffering massive headaches and joint pain. I thought maybe there was something that might help her headaches besides the pills. She has a little girl who's nine and just as cute as can be."

Sara's heart hurt for the pain the woman must be suffering, "How old is she?"

"That's the hardest part about this, Sara, she's only twenty-five years old." Both women were quiet as the implications of having cancer so young set in.

"At least she already has a child. From what I hear, the chemo and radiation make most women sterile afterwards," Sara said softly.

Grace sighed, "She's lost all of her hair and she just looks so fragile, but she's determined to take care of her little girl. From what I can tell, she's been dealing with this all alone for months."

"That is so not right!"

"I know. Jane and I talked about it and we're doing what we can for her and her little girl until she gets back on her feet. Anyway, do you happen to remember what pressure point was good for headaches?"

"Yeah. It's right between the thumbs and the first finger, deep into the webbing. Remember to squeeze hard and have her talk to you. She should feel the pressure go away once you hit the right spot. You'll have to hold it for at least ten minutes before you can release the pressure."

"Okay, now I remember. I think I can handle that."

"Grace, if she's in a lot of pain, she might need to go to the hospital..."

"She won't do it. She's a registered nurse and says that they'll only admit her and pump her full of pain drugs that take her ability to function away from her. She'd rather suffer some pain and be in control than the alternative. This was her last chemo session, and she's determined to fight this on her terms."

"I guess I can understand that," Sara said, turning as she felt someone tap her on the shoulder. She turned to see Jackson standing behind her. "Hang on a sec," she told Grace before pulling the phone from her ear.

"Ready to go?" she asked Jackson with a smile.

"Yeah. Trent is pulling the car up to the front," Jackson said, wanting to ask her about the conversation he had just overheard, but deciding to wait until they were in the car.

"Great! Let me finish up this call and I'll be right out." Sara put the phone back to her ear and said, "Grace, I need to go, but call me if you have any other questions. I don't know what help I can be long distance like this, but I'll do what I can."

"Thanks, sis. Maybe you could send up some extra prayers for her. I think she could really use them."

"I'll do that. I'll call you tomorrow night and see how things are."

"Thanks, Sara. Have a good night."

Sara pocketed the phone and then turned to see Jackson and Trent saying their farewells to Bill and his other guests. Making her way across the room, she hugged Bill tightly and thanked him for the lovely dinner. "I'll talk to you tomorrow afternoon," she smiled at him.

"The meeting's set for 2 o'clock. Feel free to bring these two along with you if they're available."

Sara smiled at Jackson and Trent and then nodded, "I'll see what I can do. I personally can't wait to see their video presentation."

"You and me both. Drive safe."

Before leaving, she pulled Pastor Jameson aside and asked him to remember Gracie's new neighbor in his evening prayers. From what Gracie had said, it sounded like the young woman needed all the help she could get.

Chapter 7

San Diego, California ...

"Grace, you have a visitor," Katelin told her the next day.

Grace looked up to see Katelin grinning at her broadly. "Where is he?" already knowing who had stopped in for a visit.

"In the auditorium. He said to tell you he wasn't going anywhere until after practice, so you didn't need to hurry down on his account."

"Thanks. Have the kids started arriving yet?" Grace asked, referring to the three hundred and some kids who would be arriving in the next fifteen minutes for choir practice. The Southern California Children's Choir had embarked on a brand new format this term thanks to the generosity of Michael's parents.

They had funded the entire season and then some, leaving Grace and her assistant more than enough time to plan and find new and exciting music. Today, they were introducing a brand new Aaron Copland piece that would be used to open their end of the term concert. The piece was one of the most difficult pieces they'd done with the group of child singers, and they would be adding choreography in as well. They only had eight weeks to get it ready for the concert, and they would need every rehearsal until then.

"There were only about twenty down there when I came up, but the bus from across town hadn't arrived yet."

"Fine. Do we need to go back over any of the movements for the first melody?" Grace asked, trying hard to remember if they'd covered everything.

"I don't think so. I went through the entire piece a while ago and it seemed like we caught everything. I just hope the kids can remember what to do."

Grace smiled, "Have some faith in our young charges. They are quicker than you think." Grace grabbed the stack of music and headed towards the auditorium, Katelin on her heels.

Choir practice went fairly smoothly, despite the fact that several of the kids appeared to be catching colds. "Now remember, we don't want everyone to get sick, so if you are still coughing on Wednesday, we want you to stay home." It wasn't often that Grace made such a request, but they already had a scheduled rehearsal off on Friday, so that would give those who were getting sick almost a week to recover before returning. "Also, please memorize the words to our new song. We want to start choreography on Monday, so it's important that everyone has the words memorized before then."

Grace and Katelin watched the kids as they all nodded their acceptance of her directions and then Katelin began their traditional "Goodbye" song. A haunting melody that had become set to the traditional Gaelic poem and had become the trademark for the choir seven years ago. It was still used to end each rehearsal, and also to say "Goodbye" to choir members who were either moving, or had become too old to participate the next year.

It was set in three-part harmony, and never failed to bring tears to the eyes of both the audience and Grace herself:

May the road rise up to meet you
May the wind be always at your back
May the sun shine warm upon your face
May the rains fall soft upon your fields
Until we meet again
And May God hold you
In the palm of his hands

As the soft melody drifted away, she closed her eyes briefly, letting the momentary silence soothe and nurture her soul. Music had always been a source of strength for her, and as she opened her eyes and dismissed her young charges, she hoped that music would be with them always.

"That always gets to me, you know," Michael's voice sounded from behind her.

Grace turned with a smile and squatted down so that she was on eye-level with him as he stood on the auditorium floor. "Yeah? Me too. What are you doing here?"

"Well, I have something to show you and was hoping you'd take a ride with me before you headed home."

Grace smiled at him and then shook her head, "I can't. I have to pick the girls up at the school," she glanced at her wristwatch, "in twenty minutes."

"What if I could get someone else to perform that task? Would you come with me then?" Michael asked, already pulling his phone from the clip on his belt.

"Well, I would have to give it serious consideration at that point."

"Done." Michael watched her with a smirk on his face, having already planned this out and only needing to give the plan a green light. "Hey, bro." Michael chuckled at something that was said and then grinned, "Sure."

Grace watched his side of the conversation, knowing she'd just been had. Michael wasn't the spur of the moment type of guy, so whatever he wanted to show her had been carefully planned out in advance.

"Okay." He pocketed the phone and then looked at her, "Now that the girls are taken care of, go grab your stuff."

Grace crossed her arms over her chest, and prepared to give him a hard time, but never got the chance. A young body slammed into her from behind, wrapping skinny arms around her legs and squeezing. "Bye, Miss Powers!"

Almost as soon as the impromptu hug began, it ended and the little body took off in a flash of energy towards the exit. Grace watched in bemusement at a mother ruffled the hair of her exuberant son, a newcomer to the choir this year, and one of the recipients of the generous grant Michael's parents had bestowed upon the choir.

"One of these days they're going to knock you right off the stage," Michael commented, reaching up and lifting her bodily off the stage. "You need to give yourself a buffer zone of six to eight feet. That way if they accidentally knock you over, you don't fall off the stage, only onto it."

Grace put her hands on Michael's shoulders as he set her down, keeping her feet inches from the ground for a moment too long. She looked into his eyes and her heart melted, as it did each time she looked at him. "What did I ever do to deserve you?" she whispered, amazed at the fullness this one man had brought to both her and her young daughter's lives.

"You must have been very, very good this year. Just think of me as an early Christmas present."

Grace chuckled as her feet finally found purchase on the ground, "Christmas was only about seven weeks ago. You're a little early, aren't you?"

"Not at all. The way I figure it, I'm a few years late. Now, enough stalling woman. Go grab your stuff and meet me out front. I want to show you something!" Michael said it with a smile and a gentle push towards the side door, which would take her upstairs to her office.

Grace managed to retrieve her purse and briefcase without getting waylaid by anyone, an amazing feat considering how many people were still in the building at this time of day. It was Monday, and that meant the symphony orchestra would be arriving soon to practice, as well as the adult chamber choir. The building was always being used for something, but Mondays always seemed to be particularly busy.

She entered the foyer of the building, not seeing Michael, and then headed out the front door. Several people were milling around outside and she waved at them, heading straight for the sleek little sports car that sat waiting by the curb.

She got into the car and then buckled up, "So tell me, where exactly we are going?"

"It's a surprise. Now, close your eyes and tell me about your day."

Grace smiled at him, but willingly played along. This playful side of Michael was one she adored, "Well, after getting Daniella ready for school, we went next door and helped Emily do the same. Victoria was feeling slightly better today, and with the exception of still suffering from a headache, she was actually up and dressed when we arrived.

"Daniella insisted on holding each and every puppy before we could leave for school. She seems to think they will remember if she ignores them and doesn't want to hurt their feelings. Oh, and she now has names for all nine of them. She and Emily seemed to have formed some sort of cooperative with the single-minded goal of driving both Tori and I into an early grave."

"What are the two princesses up to now?" Michael asked, having been witness to the 'we only want to keep three puppies' debacle from a few days ago.

Grace sighed, still keeping her eyes closed and hoping their destination wasn't much further. She'd not slept well the night before, having heard noises outside around 11 p.m. and then unable to sleep as her mind had taken a detour down the road to paranoia. She hid a yawn behind her hand.

"Tired?" Michael asked, having noticed the dark circle beneath her eyes and curious as to what had kept her from sleeping.

Grace yawned again, "Yeah. I have to tell you if I have to keep my eyes shut much longer, there is a definite possibility I may fall asleep." She felt the car stop moving as she ended her prediction and then she waited.

Michael came around to the passenger side of the car, "Keep your eyes closed for another minute or two." He gently helped her from the car, having parked where the pavement slowly climbed to meet the sidewalk so she would have less chance of stumbling.

He steered her around the building and then said, "Open your eyes."

Grace opened her eyes to see a majestic building standing in front of her. The sign on the building announced the reason for their visit. "New Home of the Simpson Pediatric Cancer Center" and she smiled before flinging herself into Michael's arms. "You did it!"

Michael grinned back and nodded his head, "Yep. Mom and dad couldn't wait to jump on board with the idea, and I've already had calls from several colleagues who want to be a part of it. By the time we're through putting everything together, this will be the premier treatment center for pediatric cancer patients in North America."

"Don't you mean the world?" Grace laughed, looking at the sign one more time in wonder.

"Well, I was trying to be modest, but – yeah! In the world. Finally, I'll have everything I need to really help sick kids get better and stay that way. I realize I can't cure everyone, but with the right combination of personnel and treatments, I can sure give them all a fighting chance."

"Michael, I'm so proud of you. I can't believe what you've managed to put together in just a few short weeks! Wow! I mean, really – just wow!" Grace leaned up and kissed Michael on the lips, intending to pull away, but he held her close and deepened the kiss before letting her go.

"Now it's my turn to say 'wow!' Grace, I know it's quick and everything is changing in my life, but I can't imagine doing this without you. I can't explain it, but you and Daniella have become a part of my life." He searched her eyes, looking for any signs that he was moving too fast. What he saw reflecting back at him made him want to shout for joy! "I think we definitely have a future together. What do you think?"

Grace looked into his eyes, amazed at full her heart was at the moment. "Michael, I know there's something happening between us, and I want to explore that..."

"But..."

"I have to be careful, not only for myself, but for Daniella. She gives her affections so easily; I couldn't bear to do anything that would eventually cause her hurt."

Michael sobered and felt his heart become even more endeared towards the lovely woman in front of him. "That is just one of the many things that draws me to you. Daniella is a true princess and I would never cause her harm. I understand that you need a little time, but I'm putting you on notice now. We have something special here and I can't wait to see where it leads us."

Grace gave him a tender smile, reaching up and laying a hand along his strong jawline, "Me too." She looked at the sign one more time and then asked, "So, when is all of this supposed to finally come together?"

"By the end of the summer. There's quite a lot of work to be done on the inside of the building. Contractors are coming next week to start the demolition work, and then another team is coming in from the east coast the week after that. Things will really be underway by the time you get back from Jane's wedding."

Grace looked at him in confusion, "By the time I get back? Aren't you coming too?"

Michael secretly pumped his fist in the air, but calmly asked, "Did you want me to? I wasn't sure..."

"Of course I want you to come along. That is, if you can get away from all of this," Grace gestured towards the building.

Michael smiled, gave her a peck on the nose and then nodded his head, "I was kind of planning to come all along, but I didn't want to assume too much. I would love to escort you to Jane and Samuel's wedding. In fact, I've already kind of commandeered my dad's private jet to fly us to Montana. If that's okay with you?"

Grace laughed and slapped him gently on the shoulder, "You've been very busy today."

"Yes, ma'am. I certainly have. Now, I believe a certain young princess is waiting at home to have a grand tea party with myself and the guest of honor –

you. When I stopped by the school earlier to speak with Brad, she was adamant that a tea party happen this evening. I kind of promised her it would."

Grace chuckled as he led her back to the car, "You and your promises. I need to hide a video camera in her room and record these events for my future viewing pleasure."

"Don't you dare! I can just see it now. The first commercial for the new facility will be a picture of me, sitting between the stuffed teddy bear and her stuffed rabbit, wearing the purple tiara and earrings, with the pink boa wrapped around my neck."

By the time he finished describing a typical dress-up outfit, required attire for one of Princess Daniella's tea parties, Grace was laughing so hard she had tears leaking from her eyes. Once she gained control of her laughter, she told him, "That would make a great ad campaign. Don't you think? Maybe the other doctors who sign on to work there could dress-up as well. You could make the tea party a weekly event for the kids that come there to be treated."

Michael looked at her in shock, "You're serious, aren't you?"

"Why not? I heard you tell Dani that laughter was sometimes the best medicine. If the staff was on board with it, it could be a weekly event that all of the kids looked forward to. You could even get some manly costume pieces. Things like crowns, and shields – you know, princely items."

The wheels began to turn in Michael's head and his smiled continued to grow as the idea took shape. "I love it! I mean, what other facility could boast of such an activity?" Michael navigated the last turn leading him back to where Grace had left her car parked, "Could you help me with the costume pieces?"

Grace shook her head, "Not me. But I just happen to know where you can find an expert in all things bling and tea party."

"Oh, that's perfect. I'll take Daniella to the costume store with me!"

Grace opened the car door, "She'd love it. You do know she will expect to be invited to each and every tea party?"

"Of course. She will be the reigning princess and in charge of making everyone else feel included. She does that really well already, and she's only four!"

"She's bossy! What you're assuming is kindness is her manipulating you until you do what she wants," Grace told him with a grin. "Are you coming back to the house to have dinner with us?"

"Yes. Brad and Teresa were stopping by to pick up a couple of take-and-bake pizzas before running the girls home. If Victoria's feeling up to it, maybe you could convince her to join us for dinner."

"I hope she is. She needs a change of scenery, that's for sure. I'll see you back at the house," Grace told him before closing the car door and jogging over to her own vehicle.

She mused about the adventure Michael was getting ready to embark upon and offered up a small prayer for its success. He was a wonderful, compassionate man, who had taken those traits and used them to help sick and hurting children. He had been wonderful with Dani when there'd been a possibility that she had leukemia, helping calm her fears in the hospital and then calming her mother's fears in the waiting room. As Grace drove home, she glanced in the rearview mirror to see Michael following right behind her. She relaxed as she replayed his comments about seeing where their relationship led. She couldn't imagine a better plan than that.

Chapter 8

Castle Peaks, Montana ...

"Mr. Mercer, what your architect has drawn up is amazing!" Jackson commented, still looking at the blueprints that had been delivered only moments before.

"Well, he had quite a bit of input from Sara and Dr. Baker. And I want you to feel free to make as many changes as you think are necessary. Oh, and call me Bill!"

Jackson nodded his head, still glued to the papers in front of him. The Mercer-Brownell Foundation was going to become the go-to place for respite care of cancer patients across the country. It would cater not only to their physical needs, but the focus would be on stabilizing their medical condition and pain so that they could get back to living. Whether that be in full remission, or only for a few more weeks. The center's main goal was to improve the quality of whatever time its patients had left.

Jackson was a realist, and he had seen firsthand how devastating cancer could be on both the patient and their extended family. Having the resources to alleviate as much pain and suffering as possible, all located in one place, was an amazing feat. One he was proud to be a part of.

"Once you're done looking at them drawings, I thought I drive you over to see the Beckett place. Dillon called this morning, and all of his siblings are in agreement to sell the place. I've already made him an offer and he's accepted it."

Jackson stared in wonder at the older gentleman standing next to him, "You bought a house?"

"Well, you can't live in the B&B forever! And if you'll remember, it is the only vacant house in fifty miles."

Jackson nodded his head, still shocked that this man had purchased a house, sight unseen. "What if the house is all rundown?"

"It isn't. Like Trent told you, the townsfolk have been keeping up with the yard work and such. It's probably a little dusty on the inside, but Sara will have that problem tackled in no time at all. In fact, a group of ladies from the church should be there now, starting to clean everything up."

"Really? I mean..."

Bill chuckled and patted the young man on the back, "Son, you might as well get used to having lots of people up in your business. It's kind of how things work around here. We're a small community and we stick together. It's just how we do things in Castle Peaks."

"I guess I'd forgotten how close knit small towns were. The town I grew up in only had about two thousand people in it. It was the largest town in eighty miles, so we had a pretty large high school since kids came from all around the area."

"Sara mentioned something about a small town up in Oregon. Do you mind my asking why you left?" Bill asked.

"I went off to med school and realized that I could help more people if I got more training."

"Sounds reasonable. Well, you ready to go see your new house?"

"Sure," Jackson replied, still trying to adjust to how quickly his life was changing. Seven days ago he'd arrived in Castle Peaks for a personal interview with Sara Harding, the director of the new Mercer-Brownell Foundation.

Since that time, he'd agreed to become the facility's medical director, had agreed to move to Castle Peaks by the first week of March, and now he was in the process of purchasing the only available house in town.

He was still musing about these things when Bill pulled his truck into the driveway of a big sprawling house. The thing was huge!

"Bill, I can't live here!" he told the older man as they both exited the truck.

"And why not?" Bill asked, seeing Sara wave at him from the large picture window. Smoke rose from the chimney and he headed towards the front porch, stamping wet snow from his feet one he reached the top.

"Well, I mean look at the place. It's way too big for one person."

Bill gave him an enigmatic stare that Jackson didn't even try to interpret and then pushed the front door open and entered.

Jackson stomped the snow from his boots and followed him inside, stopping to stare at the sight before him. A staircase, with ornate wooden rails rose on his right to the second story. A hallway led to the back of the house, directly in front of him, and to his left, a doorway opened up into a large room where a massive fireplace and hearth filled the entire far wall. Moss rock had been used to create the fireplace wall, instead of brick, giving the room a rustic feel and bringing part of nature inside.

Large log furniture was placed strategically around the room, and a large pile of white dust cloths lay on the floor near the window, having been removed by Sara and her crew of cleaning ladies.

"Jackson, what do you think? We haven't started on the upstairs yet, but everything seems to be in good condition, just a little dusty is all."

There were wooden floors throughout the house, with large area rugs in each room, underneath the furniture, and in the walkways. A large bolt protruded from the rocks in the middle of the fireplace, and Jackson pointed to it, "What's that for?"

Bill laughed when he saw where he was pointing, "You really have been in the city too long. That, my friend, is where a Bull Moose mount used to hang."

"You mean, an animal head?" Jackson asked curiously, not having thought about hunting since he was a teenager.

"Yep. Hunting's pretty big up here, but not something you have to do."

"You know, I used to hunt deer with my dad when I was younger, but then I started playing high school basketball and there was never any time."

"Well, if you want to go, we'll make time for it. I haven't been out in quite a few years, but there are some avid hunters in the town who wouldn't mind taking you along."

Jackson shook his head, "You know, I think I'll pass. I'd much rather watch them in the wild, than pull them from the freezer."

"To each his own," Bill added, "Either way, those that do hunt will be sharing their spoils with you. Being single and all, the women of the church will see it as their God-given duty to keep you fed and put a few pounds on you."

One of the women who were busy polishing the wooden railings on the staircase overheard him and hollered back, "Bill that reminds me. I made an extra loaf of banana bread this morning. It's out in the car. Be sure you take it home with you when you leave."

Bill whispered to Jackson, "See what I mean. And I have a housekeeper. They're always bringing me sweets and such. Why, if Cora wasn't around, I doubt I'd starve."

"Cora's your housekeeper?" Jackson asked, still trying to put all of the names and faces together.

"Yes, and more of a friend than anything else. I don't know what I would have done without her helping me take care of Miriam. She's a true blessing."

"I am glad you had someone there to help you. It sounds like your wife had a hard time."

"It was so much better once Sara came along. Miriam tried so hard to hide the fact that she was hurting from everyone, but Sara knew. That pressure stuff she did worked like a charm and my Miriam spent the last few days of her life lucid, smiling, and enjoying having her family around her. I couldn't ask for anything more than that."

"Sara was telling me about the technique she used. I can't wait to try it out for myself and see it in action. The ability to take pain away is a miracle in itself."

"That it is," Bill murmured.

"Hey, Jackson, come on over here."

Jackson followed the sound of Sara's voice to find her standing in front of a set of double doors that led to a backyard covered in snow. There was a huge tree in the middle of the yard, and in that tree was a colorful treehouse, complete with a ladder, swing, and...box?

"What's with the wooden box?" he asked, feeling silly for asking.

"That's so the kids don't try to climb with stuff in their hands. Trent explained it all to me earlier today when he let us in. There's a pulley system in the floor of the treehouse, and the kids can raise or lower the box with the rope so they can use both hands to climb the ladder."

"That's a great idea! This backyard is a kids' paradise!"

"That it is." She pointed out several other features of the backyard, hidden from view by the three feet of snow that still blanketed everything in white. "So, what do you think?"

"I can't believe I'm going to live here. The largest apartment I've lived in since leaving home was about six hundred square feet, and came with neighbors on all side except one. It was noisy, there was no privacy, and no room!"

Sara smiled at him, "Glad you like it. Now, I'm going to leave you in Bill's capable hands. Trent asked me to stop by the office before I head home, and I haven't quite mastered driving on these roads in the dark."

"Drive careful," Jackson called to her as she said her farewells to the other ladies and Bill. He looked around the small treehouse and then began to explore. An hour later, he came back down to the main floor to see Bill sitting at the kitchen table, having a cup of coffee and eating a slice of pie with the other ladies.

"This place is simply amazing. And the furniture is fantastic. Do you think Dillon would be interested in selling some of it?"

Bill looked up, "What? What are you talking about?"

"The furniture. I'm interested in buying some of it."

Bill laughed, "Son, you own *all* of it. It came with the house."

Jackson was stunned once again, "Really? They don't want any of it?"

"They took everything they wanted right after the funeral. A moving company came in and packed up all of their parent's personal affects, and the rest was to be sold with the house when the time came. That time is now."

Jackson sat down in a vacant chair at the table, nodding his thanks when one of the ladies placed a slice of pie and a cup of coffee in front of him. He couldn't believe the blessings that just kept coming his way. He turned and looked back at the large living room once more and then grinned. He was the proud owner of a fabulously furnished house.

Bill had informed him on the drive over that the house was to be considered part of his compensation and bonus package. Jackson had never been treated so well in his life, but he wasn't about to start complaining. His future was in Castle Peaks and even though the sky outside was grey with more snow clouds, the sun was shining up ahead and spring would be arriving soon.

The circle of life was about to give birth to a brand new chapter in his life and bring hope to countless others. He truly was blessed and couldn't wait to pass those blessings along to the needy souls that would be making use of the clinic's resources.

He waited to call his family until he returned to the B&B and was happy to see how excited they were for him. He'd always had the support of a loving set of parents and several siblings. He was the only one that had left Oregon, but it was all going to pay off now. The only thing that would make this move perfect was if he wasn't still going to be alone, once it was completed.

Chapter 9

S *an Diego, California, one week later...*

"Close your eyes," Michael said as he steered Grace along the sidewalk. He'd picked Grace up for lunch, making her close her eyes before he'd taken the highway out of town, which led to their current destination. A sense of déjà vu swamped Grace as she did what he requested. *What does he have up his sleeve this time?* Anticipation had a soft smile forming on her lips as she relaxed into the soft leather of the car seat. Now, they had arrived at their destination, and she still had her eyes closed, trusting him to see to her safety and her happiness as she let him move her along the soft ground.

Over the last week, Michael had been busy making plans for the new pediatric cancer clinic, and Grace had been consumed with the children's choir and helping out her new neighbor. Tori and her daughter had become part of Grace's family, eating several meals a week with them, and Emily and Dani were becoming very close.

Grace smiled as she thought about the afternoon the day before. She'd gone looking for the girls after having helped Tori try on one of the wigs that had arrived earlier that day. She'd found both girls in the backyard, sitting on a blanket, surrounded by nine bundles of fur.

Emily had been reading Daniella one of the many books she had brought home from the school library and Dani had been gazing up at her in pure admiration. There was a five-year age gap between the two children, but Daniella didn't seem to mind. Emily had become her newest idol and she imitated her every action. It was cute and really drove home the fact that Daniella needed a little brother or sister of her own.

Grace had been so lost in her thoughts, she almost opened her eyes when Michael stopped walking and turned her around to her left. He positioned her carefully, wanting her to see everything at first glance, and then quietly murmured in her ear, "Open your eyes."

Grace cracked her eyes open and then gasped. She looked at the scene before her and felt tears come to her eyes. Michael had brought her back to the spot by the lake where they'd had their first lunch date, but instead of a blanket and a picnic basket, an elegantly set table set for two awaited them. "Michael...how did you do all of this?"

Deep red roses graced the center of the table, and soft music floated around them, coming from a hidden stereo. Grace approached the table in wonder, seeing the covered dishes and the bottle of what looked like champagne chilling in a bucket of ice upon the table.

Turning back, she saw Michael watching her with a smile upon his face. "How did you do all of this?"

"I had some help," he offered, approaching her with a gleam in his eye. He pulled her into his arms, he kissed her for several moments before releasing her and suggesting, "We should eat before it gets cold."

Grace was still in shock, but allowed him to lead her to a chair where he helped her be seated. He popped the cork on the bottle, and she was pleased to see that instead of champagne, it was only chilled sparkling cider. Grace didn't really care for the taste of champagne, having not even finished the glass at her first wedding.

Michael poured them both a glass, using the crystal goblets on the table and then handed her one. "To the future." He touched his glass to hers and then watched as she slowly brought the glass to her lips and took a sip.

He was watching her so intently, she was starting to wonder why, when something caught her attention. Taking her glass away from her lips, she held it up at eye level and then gasped. Sitting in the bottom of the glass was a diamond solitaire ring.

When she looked up to find Michael, he was on bent knee, watching her intently, "Grace, would you do me the honor of agreeing to be my wife?"

Grace stared at him with an open mouth and then whispered, "Isn't this too soon? I mean, we've only known each other a few weeks."

Michael looked at her with love shining in his eyes and then took the glass from her trembling fingers. He tipped the glass, retrieving the ring with the tines of a fork and then rinsed it off in the carefully concealed bowl of ice water sitting on the side of the table.

Drying it off with a napkin, he held it up for her inspection, "Grace, I don't need months, or even years, to know that I want to spend the rest of my life with you by my side. I want to be a father to Daniella. I want to raise a family with you."

Grace couldn't keep the tears from overflowing her eyes and running down her cheeks. "Michael, I... I don't know what to say."

"Say 'Yes' for now. Everything else can be worked out, just say that you'll be my wife." Michael searched her eyes, willing her to give him some indication she was of the same mind.

Grace couldn't speak as the tears clogged her throat so she nodded her head.

Michael whooped once and then pulled her from her chair, tumbling backwards as they both fell to the soft grass in laughter. "You won't regret it. I'm going to make you the happiest woman in the world."

"I already am," Grace informed him as she watched him place the diamond solitaire upon her left hand. "You know Daniella is going to be ecstatic, right?"

"I hope so. And you don't have to answer right now, but sometime in the future, I would love to become her father. Legally."

Grace's heart was so full of love for the man in front of her. "You know, after Alec died, there was a part of me that wanted to die as well. But then I had Daniella to keep me waking up each morning, and going through the motions of life, and slowly things went back to normal.

Up until a few weeks ago, I hadn't realized I needed something else for me. When I saw Samuel and Jane growing closer together, I was jealous. Just a little bit. I missed having that connection with another adult; being able to share the day's accomplishments and challenges with someone else at the end of the day."

Michael caressed a hand down her hair; giving her all of his attention. "I want those same things. It won't always be sunshine and roses. There are days when I want to raise my fists to the sky and scream at God for taking yet another child from this earth."

"I'll be there to share your sorrow when that happens," Grace promised him, sealing her words with a tender kiss. As they broke apart, the dampness of the grass penetrated her mind and she shivered, "You are going to have a gigantic wet spot on your backside."

Michael grinned at her, giving her a push to help her rise from the ground and then standing up himself. He dusted his pants off to the best of his ability, and when he looked over his shoulder, he was indeed sporting a giant wet spot on the back of his dress pants and down his right leg. "It's a good thing I wore dark pants today. Let's eat."

Grace resumed her seat, and they spent the next forty-five minutes consuming the delicious meal that Jane and her new staff had prepared for them. "So, did Jane know what you were up to?"

Michael blushed, "Yes. I had to take her into my confidence, otherwise, I wasn't quite sure how I was going to get the ring into the glass."

"Thank you for making this moment so special," Grace told him, reaching across the table and taking his hand in hers.

Michael lifted their clasped fingers to his mouth, kissing her fingers lightly before setting her hand back down on the table. "So, I was thinking of a way we might tell Daniella the good news."

"Really? I'm all ears," Grace told him, finishing her meal and then pushing the plate back on the table."

"I was thinking of getting her a locket and having both Alec and my name engraved on it. One on each side. I don't want her to ever forget Alec."

Grace burst into tears again, "Michael that is the sweetest, most caring thing I think I've ever heard."

Michael looked at her indulgently and then leaned forward to whisper, "Are you going to cry every time I do something nice for you?"

Grace promptly nodded her head. "Yes!"

Michael sighed and then pulled a handkerchief from his pocket; Grace had already used the napkins to wipe up her tears from earlier. "Well then, I guess I better invest in some more of these," he said as he handed it across the table to her.

Grace laughed through her tears, "Either that or I need to start carrying a big box of tissues around with me." She wiped her tears, pleased when she didn't see any mascara marks on the white linen.

"So, the locket is a go?" Michael asked.

"Definitely."

"Good, let's go," he said, standing up from the table and then leading her back to the car.

"Where?" Grace asked, laughing as he hurried them along.

"To the jewelry store. I want to give it to her tonight, and if we're there before 2 o'clock, Tom promised to have it engraved before he closes this evening."

"My, my," Grace told him as he helped her into the car, "you have been busy."

"Just covering all of my bases. Why don't you start going over that very busy schedule of yours and pick a wedding date."

Grace opened her mouth and then promptly closed it as he shut her door and jogged around to the driver's side. "Really? You want me to just pick a date out of thin air?"

"No. I want to take a two week vacation with Daniella after the wedding, so pick a date when you can get away for that long."

"That's easy then. June. Anytime in June. I usually take the entire month off to decompress between one choir season and then next."

"Done. June it is. I should probably warn you – my mom is going to make a big deal out of this. Brad and Teresa have said numerous times if they had to do it over, they'd elope. I don't have the heart to do that to my mom, so we might as well enjoy the fuss."

Grace laughed, "I think I can do that. Alec and I just had a simple wedding at the base. A little fuss this time won't be too much of a hardship."

"I'm going to remind you of that a month from now when you're ready to run off to Las Vegas."

"Not going to happen. I want a church wedding with all of the trimmings. Do you think Pastor Harris would marry us?"

"I'm sure he would. Why don't you call and ask him tomorrow?" Michael said, referring to the pastor of the small church Grace attended on a regular basis.

Michael and his family had been attending a larger church, but Michael had readily switched, saying he liked the feel of the small congregation and felt at home there. Grace smiled all the way back into town. Valentine's Day was just two more days away, and for the first time in several years, she was actually looking forward to the holiday.

Chapter 10

C astle Peaks, Montana, later that night...

"Sara?" Trent called out as he entered the house by the backdoor. He entered the kitchen and sniffed appreciatively at the pot on the stove. Chili! Yum!

"Sara?" he called again, heading into the large family room and still not seeing her. Her car was in the driveway, so she had to be here somewhere. He'd gotten a message from Becky that Sara had stopped by the sheriff's office looking for him. She'd looked like she'd been crying, but hadn't seemed upset.

He looked through the house, but still didn't see her. "Sara?!" he hollered one more time, and then he heard the crash from the garage. It was used more for the storage of things, rather than cars, and he headed in that direction.

"Sara?" he called out as he opened the door between the mudroom and the garage.

"Over here. Can you come take this box before I drop it?" her voice called out.

Trent glanced to where the voice had come from and then he spotted her. She was standing on a makeshift stool, holding a box aloft with one hand, while she tried to remove the one sitting underneath it. "Sugar, what in the world are you doing? Get down from there."

"But I need this box out." Sara spared him a glance and then nodded her head towards the box she was holding up, "If you could just hold this box for a minute, I can pull the other one out."

Trent reached up and took hold of the indicated box, lifting it above his head and watching her carefully as she extricated the box beneath it. "What's so important that you needed to risk your neck to get it?"

"My mom's wedding dress," Sara informed him triumphantly when the box slid free. She started to step down from her stool, and Trent dropped the box above his head and swooped her up into his arms. Box and all.

"Hey! Put me down," she giggled.

"You are a menace to my peace of mind." Trent carried her to the open area and then put her down on her feet, "Why are you looking for your mom's wedding dress? We're already married, or do I need to remind you again."

Sara blushed and shook her head at him, "Oh, you haven't heard the news! Gracie's getting married!" Sara bounced up and down in her excitement.

"To the doctor?" Trent asked, following his wife into their home and closing the door to the garage.

"Yes! He asked her today. She called me while she was waiting to pick up Daniella and Emily from school and told me all about it. He..."

"Whoa! Slow down a minute. Who is Emily?" Trent asked, trying to keep up with the conversation, but she was talking a mile a minute.

"Emily is the neighbor's daughter. She goes to the same school as Daniella, so Grace has been taking them to school and then picking them up."

"Oh! Alright, then. Continue," Trent said as he followed her down the hall to their bedroom. He watched as Sara carefully undid the tape on the box and lifted out a plastic wrapped parcel. It was sealed to prevent any air from entering the bag in an effort to preserve the garment contained within.

Sara gingerly lifted out the satin garment with the seed pearls decorating the bodice and laid the beautiful dress out on the bed. Her mother and Grace were about the same size, with Gracie being about an inch shorter. The costumer where Grace worked had offered to oversee the alterations when Grace had mentioned being married in her mother's old dress.

Sara had thought it a wonderful idea and had promised to locate the dress and send it out right away. Sara smoothed her hand over the dress and tried to envision her mother wearing it. She'd only been a small child when her father had suddenly collapsed from a heart attack. He hadn't survived, but somehow her mother had managed to raise two little girls by herself.

She'd seen pictures of her father, but she didn't really have any true memories of the man. She took a breath and then looked up to see Trent watching her. She gave him a smile and then began packing the dress back into the box.

"So, how are you planning on getting the dress out to her?" Trent asked.

"Well, I was thinking I could send it out tomorrow in the mail, but now I'm thinking the box is too big."

"I agree. That box is too big for the normal mail to handle. Didn't you say Jackson lives in San Diego?"

Sara looked up and then nodded her head, "That's perfect. He's flying out tomorrow. Maybe he could take this as a piece of checked baggage?"

"I'm sure he wouldn't mind. I tell you what, why don't we go have some of that delicious chili I saw on the stove and then I'll drive you back into town with the dress?"

Sara laughed, "You would say anything right now in order to eat, wouldn't you?"

"You know it." Trent turned her around and started steering her back to the kitchen, "I didn't have lunch. Jeb called first thing this morning and I spent the morning helping him unclog his rain gutters. They'd completely frozen over and the water was starting to pool under the roof."

"Is everything okay?" Sara asked as she served up two bowls of the chili, added cheese and sour cream and then carried them to the table. She smiled at Trent as he removed the corn bread from the oven and then carried the hot dish over to the table with a knife and the butter.

"We won't know the answer to that question until everything starts to thaw out. We could see where the ice had heaved the seam between two panels on the roof, but whether or not it compromised the integrity of the water seal, we'll just have to wait and see."

"I hope everything's alright. When does the world start to thaw out around here? Bill keeps talking about breaking ground as soon as it thaws out, but we got another foot of snow two days ago." Sara sounded disgruntled and Trent laughed.

"I promise we do have all four seasons here. Winter just seems to hang around some years. By April, things will look much different."

"April? It's not really going to snow until April. Is it?"

Trent thought about teasing her, but then saw the depressed look on her face and chuckled, "Maybe up high in the mountains, but down here we should start warming up soon. Promise," he told her when she didn't look as if she believed him.

Sara nodded her head and then went back to eating. *Snow until April? She might as well have moved to Alaska!*

• • ◦❧◦ • •

"SO, YOU WANT ME TO deliver your mother's wedding dress to your sister, who lives in San Diego?" Jackson asked, just clarifying the late night visit from Sara and her husband.

"That's right. Her address is written on that piece of paper, as is her phone number. I'll call her tomorrow and let her know that you'll be bringing it by in the next day or so."

Jackson looked at the address and tried to place the part of town Sara's sister lived in. It was towards the beach, and in a fairly newly developed part of the city. "Okay, I guess I can do that. I take it she's getting married?"

Sara beamed at his astuteness, "Yes! She just got engaged today! Hey! You need to meet her fiancé. He's a pediatric oncologist and is getting ready to open up a new kid's cancer treatment center in San Diego. You two would have a lot in common, I bet."

"Maybe I'll get a chance to do that. I had dinner with Bill tonight, and I'm planning on coming back up here around the first week of March. I'll be driving, so a lot of the timing will depend upon the weather."

Trent nodded, "Give us a call when you head out. There's a lot of highway between here and there and a lot of mountains to cross."

Jackson nodded, "I'm looking forward to it. It's been a few years since I spent any time in the mountains."

"Be careful," Sara cautioned him. "One of these days I'll tell you about my first time driving in the mountains and the snow."

Trent smiled at her, "I think you should save that for another time. The man has a 6 a.m. flight and needs to get some rest."

"Oh! Sorry. Well, I can't wait until you're back here. The ladies and I will finish getting the house all squared away while you're gone."

Jackson hid a yawn and nodded, "Thank you for everything. Both of you. I finally feel like maybe I've found a place where I can put down roots and grow."

Sara hugged him. A trait she had come to realize was as natural to her as breathing. She hugged everyone. He returned the gesture and then shook hands with Trent.

"Have a safe trip."

"I will. See you in a couple of weeks."

Chapter 11

San Diego, California, Valentine's Day...

S   "Mommy, I can't find my rainbow shoes again," Dani hollered through the house.

"They're on the back porch," Grace hollered back, trying to finish her makeup before Michael arrived. It was Valentine's Day, and she and Michael were double dating with Jane and Samuel. Tori had insisted on keeping the girls for the evening and Grace had reluctantly agreed.

Tori had suffered a minor setback in her recovery by developing a chest cold, but she had started a rigorous course of antibiotics and her fever was gone now, so everyone had agreed that she could probably handle the two little girls for a few hours.

Armed with a bag full of dress-up accessories, Dani presented herself at the bathroom door moments later. "I's ready to go," she announced.

Grace looked at her daughter in the mirror and struggled not to laugh at the picture she presented. Daniella marched to her own drum, and for the last several months it had been playing a coronation procession. She was determined to be a princess and had outdone herself this evening.

Wearing her favorite Disney Princess nightgown, over a pair of brightly striped leggings, and her favorite rainbow tennis shoes, she was a burst of color that was almost shocking to the eyes.

She had pulled out all the stops on the *bling* factor and was adorned as any self-respecting princess should be: tiara, earrings, necklace, multiple bracelets, boa, and her most recent acquisition – sparkle pretend makeup.

Per Grace's suggestion, Michael and Dani had made a trip to the largest costume store in the San Diego area in search of proper tea party accessories. It had been the first outing where Michael and Dani had gone without her, and he definitely needed to learn to set boundaries with the little girl. Soon.

Not only had she convinced him to purchase every prince and princess costume the store had, but then she had discovered the makeup section of the store and fallen in love. The store clerk had used the word "pretend" when referring to the non-toxic makeup and Michael had willingly bought her the largest kit they offered.

That was several days earlier, and Dani hadn't left the house since that time without having bright blue or purple sparkle makeup smeared across her eyes. Luckily, the stuff washed off skin with a little soap and water. Grace was only praying it did the same with towels, bed sheets, and the carpet.

"Dani, don't you think you might have just a little too much makeup on for visiting Tori and Emily?" Grace asked, biting the inside of her lip to keep from laughing.

"Princesses can't never has too much makeup on. The lady at the costume store had makeup all over her arms and stuff. I's just put it on my face!"

Grace closed her eyes and groaned. Evidently, Michael had forgotten to mention that the store clerk was heavily tattooed. *Lord, please don't let her start wanting one of those. She's only four!*

"Well, I'm sure the clerk was much older than you are. Wearing paint on your arms and legs is something reserved for adults."

"Unhuh," her daughter informed her. "Billy has paint on his arm. He showed it to me at recess. He said his grandpa gave it to him and he licked the paper and then rubbed it really hard on his arm and the picture showed up. It was a turtle."

Grace nodded her head, "A turtle, huh? That sounds interesting." Changing the subject, she turned the light off in the bathroom and headed towards the kitchen, "Grab your things and I'll walk you over to Tori's house."

Grace and Daniella crossed the grass between the two yards, going through the back gate to see Emily playing with the puppies. "Hey Dani, come help me. These guys won't leave me alone."

Grace laughed as her daughter dropped her bag and ran to help. *At least she doesn't have those plastic shoes on tonight!* She watched for a moment as the puppies spied a new playmate and stumbled across each other and the grass towards Daniella.

Hearing laughter, she spied Tori sitting on the back patio, with a blanket draped over her shoulders, "Hey, should you be out here?"

Tori smiled, "I'm fine. Believe it or not, I'm tired of being cooped up inside the house all day. Besides, the air is warm enough and I haven't had a fever since yesterday. The antibiotics seem to be doing the trick."

"Good to know." Grace dropped Dani's backpack next to the door and then sat down in the only other chair.

"Do I dare ask what Dani has all over her face?" Tori questioned with a grin.

"Michael took her with him to the costume store and they found some 'fake' makeup that sparkles. He bought her the biggest package they had and she's determined to wear all of it before the month's out."

Tori laughed, "I remember when Emily went through that stage, except I came home from working a split shift, and the babysitter assured me she was sleeping soundly. The little scamp had snuck out of her bedroom and was happily, albeit very quietly, trying out every shade of lipstick and eye shadow she could get opened."

Grace giggled, "How old was she?"

"Four – about the same age as Dani. The really bad part was that school pictures were the next day, and no matter how much cold cream or makeup remover I used, I couldn't get it all off. Luckily, the school offered retakes a few weeks later." Tori laughed as she remembered the teacher and other parents' expressions when she dropped Emily off the next day for school. It had not been a pretty sight!

"Well, at least this stuff comes off skin with soap and water. I haven't tried to get it of the carpet or the towels yet, I'm waiting until this weekend."

"Good luck with that." Tori looked up and waved at Michael as he entered the backyard, "Hi, Michael. Come to steal your valentine away?"

"Don't you know it!" Michael paused as Dani came running across the yard and threw herself into his arms, "Hey, squirt! I see you're making good use of the makeup."

"Mommy doesn't like it," Dani pouted, before casting a glance in her mother's direction.

"Now, Dani, that's not entirely true. I simply suggested maybe we only try out one color at a time. You don't want to use all of your pretty make up. Do you?"

"Oh, it's okay, mommy. I's knows where to buy more."

The adults all laughed at the seriousness of her expression and the fact that in her mind, running out simply meant you needed to visit the store and pick more up. *Gonna have to work on that!*

"Well, I think you look gorgeous. Now, it appears that your adoring fans await you, Princess Dani. We'll see you after a bit." Michael kissed the top of her head, avoiding the tiara and the sparkly eye shadow and then set her back down on her feet.

"Ready to go?" he asked Grace, wrapping an arm around her waist.

"Yes. Tori, are you sure you feel up to this?"

"Quit worrying about me and go enjoy yourselves. The girls and I have the latest animated movie to watch, and a pizza on its way."

"Have fun," Michael called out to the girls as he led Grace from the backyard. "Quit worrying! They'll be fine. Tori looks much better, and she is a nurse. If she can't make a judgment call about her own health, I don't know who can."

. . ⚬ɬᴐ . .

THE SYMPHONY CONCERT and dinner at The Inferno had been perfect, as had the company. Jane and Samuel were getting married in exactly one month, back in Castle Peaks, and Grace and Michael announced they would be tying the knot on June second. Grace's last concert of the season was scheduled for May 26th, and that would provide her with approximately a week to stress over the final wedding details.

"So, is your future mother-in-law in wedding bliss?" Jane asked, having met Michael's mother on several occasions and figuring her for the type that would find wedding planning paradise.

"Don't you know it! But I'm really okay with that. She's handling all of the details in regards to the reception, and the food, and such. Speaking of wedding details, will you stand up with me?"

Jane smiled, "Really?" When Grace nodded, Jane hugged her, "I'd love to. And you just let me know what you need my help with."

"What are you two girls talking about over there?" Samuel asked as he and Michael returned to their table.

"Jane's just agreed to be a bridesmaid in our wedding," Grace told Samuel as Michael leaned down and kissed her on the cheek.

"That's wonderful!" Both men sat down and then Samuel commented, "It's funny how quickly life can change, isn't it?"

All the others nodded their heads in agreement.

• • ❧ • •

"AUNT TORI, I CAN'T find my green tiara," Dani whined as she pawed through the various costume pieces she'd just dumped onto the floor of the living room.

"I'm sure you just forgot it at home, sweetie. The purple one you're wearing looks gorgeous."

"It's not for me. It's for you. It matches your eyes. You have to wear the green one!" Dani placed her hands on her hips and nodded her head.

Tori laughed and then assured her, "I think I can live without wearing a tiara tonight. Why don't we put in and eat some popcorn?"

Dani shook her head, "No! I want to go find the green tiara!"

Tori saw the tantrum beginning to brew in the little girl's eyes and cringed. She was feeling better, but not quite up to a Dani tantrum. Throwing a beseeching look at her daughter, she asked, "Emily, could you walk Dani home and help her find the green tiara while I get the popcorn ready?"

"Sure, momma. Come on, Dani. Let's go find your tiara." Tori watched the girls as they headed out the backdoor and then shook her head. She glanced at the clock on the wall and figured it shouldn't take them any longer than about five minutes to walk next door, find the missing tiara, and walk back.

Tori put the first bag of popcorn in the microwave and then loaded up the DVD. After cooking the second bag, she looked out the back window, expecting to see the girls by the puppies, but there weren't any little girls in the backyard.

Growing concerned when she glanced at the clock and fifteen minutes had gone by, she slipped her sandals on and headed through the backyard to go find them. She was having a pretty good day, but knew that she would pay for over-exerting herself tomorrow.

Stopping to catch her breath at the gate, she was surprised to see a sleek orange Mustang sitting in Grace's driveway. *I wonder whose car that is.* She started across the grass, stopping several times when the world started to spin crazily, praying for enough strength to find the girls and get back home.

After the third pause, she looked up to see the silhouette of a man standing on Grace's front porch. *So that's who the car belongs to.* Forcing herself to stand up straight, she slowly made her way across the remaining grass, wondering if the girls had gotten distracted, or if maybe they were hiding inside from the stranger.

As she stepped up onto the porch, he turned and speared her with his dark green eyes. His dark hair fell over his forehead and she had the strangest urge to reach up and put it back into place. There was a large cardboard box standing next to him and she wondered if he was a delivery boy, or something else.

"Hi," she offered softly. "Can I help you?"

The man smiled, revealing perfectly straight teeth, and that's when she saw the dimple in his left cheek. He looked kind of familiar, and she tried to figure out where she'd seen him before, but nothing came to mind. "Are you Grace Powers?"

"Afraid not," Tori said, leaning against the railing of the porch as another wave of dizziness swamped her.

"Hey! Are you okay?" the man asked, narrowing his eyes at her in concern.

Tori waved his concern off, "Sure. Just a little dizzy is all. Grace isn't home, but I could sign for the delivery if you like."

"Sign?" he asked in confusion.

Tori was prevented from answering when she spied two little bodies slithering across the grass, "Excuse me for a moment." She turned and called to the girls, "Emily! Dani! Come here!"

Both little girls popped their heads up and then gave her relieved smiles as they stood to their feet and ran to where she was attempting to stay upright. They both started chattering as soon as they reached her.

"We was sneaking back to avoid the strange man."

"Why are you talking to the strange man, Aunt Tori? Momma says we're not supposed to talk to strangers. I was showing Emily hows we snucked out when the bad men tried to take me."

The chattering continued, and in the midst of it, Tori realized that at some point in the recent past, Grace and Dani had been involved in something abnormal. She made a mental note to ask Grace about that at her next opportunity.

Finally feeling the last of her strength leave her, she held her hand up, effectively silencing both girls. "Emily, the popcorn is all ready for your movie. Why don't you take Dani and head on back? I'll be there in a few minutes."

Emily nodded her head and grabbed Dani's hand, pulling her along. "Come on, Dani. Let's go find the green earrings."

Chapter 12

Tori watched both girls until they entered the backyard and then she pulled up all of the strength she could muster before turning to face the stranger once again. "Sorry about that. Uhm, maybe you could just push Grace's package up next to the door and she'll be sure to see it when she gets home."

"I don't think I should do that."

Grace closed her eyes. *He was going to be difficult!* Taking a breath, she stared at him, using the look that had gotten compliance from more than one difficult patient, but on him it had absolutely no effect. "Look, I'm not feeling very well, so could you just leave the box and go. Grace will be home later tonight and I'll make sure she knows it's sitting here?"

"Are you ill?" the man asked as he looked her over with a critical eye.

Grace felt like a bug under a microscope. She knew what she looked like at the moment. She was rail thin, her face had a grey pallor to it, she was wearing an oversize sweatshirt that completely hid the shape of her body, or the lack thereof. She had made a concession and was wearing one of the wigs Grace and Jane had convinced her to buy, but other than a perfectly fake head of hair, she looked like something the cat had not only dragged home, but through the wringer first.

"You know what, do whatever you want with that box. If you leave your name and number on the door, I'm sure Grace will contact you and arrange for you to bring it back." With that said, Tori carefully navigated her way down the two steps and started across the grass.

When she reached the large maple tree in the middle of the two yards, she stopped and leaned against it as she surveyed the remaining distance she still needed to cross. *I'm never going to make it!* Tears of frustration filled her eyes, and she bowed her head in defeat as she realized she only had two choices. Try to make it to the backyard before she collapsed and hope that Emily wouldn't be too scared when she found her. Or, stay by the tree until Grace came home. They would most likely be gone a few more hours, and maybe she'd find enough strength to make it back inside the house before then.

She was so deep in her thoughts, she didn't realize the strange man had followed her progress across the yard, first with his eyes, and then with his long legs.

"Ma'am?" he asked startling her and causing her to shriek in alarm. "Sorry. I didn't mean to startle you, but you look like you need some help."

"I'm...," Tori tried to tell him she was fine, but she wasn't! The tears flowed faster now and she just shook her head, unable to verbalize the frustration she was feeling at the moment. The respiratory infection had compromised her ability to breathe deeply, causing her oxygen levels to hover at barely acceptable levels when she was sitting up in bed. They certainly weren't able to support any type of activity and she'd known that when she'd gone searching for the girls.

"Hey, I know you don't know me from Adam, but I'm a doctor. I take it you live next door?"

Tori nodded and tried to stem the flow of tears.

"Good. Well, I have a very important package for Grace from her sister, Sara, up in Montana. Their mom's wedding dress is in that box and I really don't think I should leave it sitting on the front porch. And frankly, you don't look like you've got enough energy to make it back inside the house. How about I help you inside, and then I can leave the dress with you until Grace gets home?"

Tori watched him and tried to determine why he seemed so familiar. *I know I've seen him before, but where?* "You're a doctor?"

He nodded, "Jackson Myers, at your service."

Tori looked at him and cocked her head to the side. *Jackson? Wasn't that the name of Michelle's boyfriend in high school?* She looked him over once again and then shrugged her shoulders, "Tori. Sure you're not a murderer?"

Jackson smiled and then asked, "Would I tell you if I were?"

Tori shook her head, "No, probably not." Deciding he had just presented her with the only viable alternative, given her situation, she gave him a small smile, "If you could help me back to the house I would really appreciate it."

Jackson nodded and then offered her his arm to lean against, "So, you've been sick?"

"You might say that. I just finished the last of my chemo and lucky me, I got a respiratory infection as a going away present."

Jackson digested the fact that the fragile woman hanging onto his arm had just survived cancer. "Shall I tell you what my specialty is?" he asked as he helped her navigate the narrow gate.

"Sure. Why not? We have to talk about something, don't we?"

Jackson admired the snarky attitude and figured it had probably served her well during her treatment. "I treat people with cancer. In fact, I'm going to be heading up a new facility in Montana with Grace's sister that will provide out-of-the-box alternatives to traditional medicine."

"What kind of treatments?" Tori asked, struggling for breath as she tried not to step on the first puppy to come barreling up against her legs. "Sorry about the pups."

"Goodness, there's a bunch of them," Jackson said, trying not to step on the wiggling bodies that were jumping and vying for attention from the newcomers.

Tori smiled and then told him, "Nine. They're almost nine weeks old and ready to find new homes. Want one? Or nine?"

Jackson laughed, "Uh, no. I'm not in the market for a dog right now. I'm moving to an entirely new place in a few weeks, and two days ago there was about three feet of snow in the backyard of the house I'm going to be living in." Jackson still couldn't get his head wrapped around the fact that the house was being thrown in as part of his compensation package.

"Three feet of snow?" Tori got a smile upon her face, "We used to have snow where I lived when I was growing up. Sometimes I miss it."

"I grew up with snow, but not as much as they have in Montana. It's going to take some getting used to." They had reached the back patio and Tori sank down in one of the chairs.

"Thanks for the help."

"No problem. Let me run get the box and I'll bring it back over and then get out of your hair." Jackson really wished he had his medical bag with him. Tori, as she'd introduced herself, didn't look good at all.

Retrieving the box, he hurried back across the yards, alarmed when he saw Tori struggling to breathe. There was a blue tinge around her mouth, and it was obvious she was in respiratory distress.

Squatting down next to her chair, he grabbed her wrist and began measuring her heart rate, nodding when it registered slow but steady. "Tori, you need some medical help. Where's your phone?"

"No...oxygen...I..." she struggled to tell him and he finally figured out what she was saying.

Opening the backdoor, he spied the two girls lounging in front of the TV and called for their assistance. "Hey ladies, could one of you come here and help me for a minute?"

Emily glanced out the back door and then ran towards her mother. Jackson stopped her and calmly asked, "Sweetie, she's having a little trouble breathing. Does she have an oxygen bottle around here somewhere?"

Emily looked at her mom and then nodded, "In the bedroom. It's on wheels."

"Great! You stay here with her and I'll be right back." Jackson headed in the direction the little girl had looked and moments later returned with the green oxygen bottle and mask.

Fitting it over Tori's mouth and nose, he turned it on and then instructed her to breathe nice and slow, "That's it. Again." He watched as the blue tinge disappeared around her mouth and she was taking nice, deep breaths once again.

After about fifteen minutes, he removed the mask and took her pulse again. The capillary refill response on her fingernails was back to normal and he was pleased to see the crisis had passed.

Tori thanked him with her eyes and then turned her attention to the two little girls who were clinging to her knees, "Hey, why don't you two go finish your movie. I'm okay, I just walked a little too far."

"Aunt Tori, I's sorry..."

"Dani, you've nothing to be sorry about. Go watch your movie while I say 'Goodnight' to Mr. Jackson."

The girls hugged her and then scooted back inside the house. She watched them for a moment and then lifted one of the puppies into her lap. She needed something to hold onto and the warm body was comforting.

Looking up, she met Jackson's green eyes and once again felt like she'd met him before. "Thank you."

"Are you sure I don't need to call your doctor?"

Tori smiled at him, "I'm a registered nurse, and yes, I'm sure. Before I got sick, I worked on the oncology floor. I knew I didn't have the strength to walk next door, but the girls had been gone too long."

"That's my fault. I think I scared them when I rang the doorbell. I could hear them inside and waited around hoping they would open the door so the dress could sit inside."

"Well, the dress is safe with me. Grace will be back shortly and I'll see that she gets it."

"Shall I place it inside the house?" Jackson asked.

"Yes. Could you sit it by the front door?"

Jackson picked up the box and nodded, "Sure." He carried the box inside, noticing the many pictures on the walls and stopped to look at them on his way back. What he saw made his heart stop. He glanced back out the door and then back at the pictures on the wall.

When he felt something next to his leg, he noticed the older of the two girls was standing next to him. She pointed at a picture of an older woman and said, "That's my grandma. She's in heaven."

Jackson nodded his head and then walked back to the patio, "I noticed the pictures on the wall in your living room."

Tori smiled, "Yeah. Most of them are of my mom and sister. They were both killed in a car crash right around the time Emily was born."

"I'm sorry for your loss. It must have been hard caring for a newborn and grieving at the same time."

Tori nodded, "It was the most difficult time in my life. But Emily gave me a reason to go on, so I did."

Jackson looked at the little girl and then back to her mother. "How old is she?"

"Nine. And I'm twenty-five, even though I know I must look forty at the moment."

"No, I..."

"It's okay. I look in the mirror. But I'm on the road to recovery now. No more chemo. No more radiation. Each day I get stronger, and soon this will all be nothing but a bad memory."

"You sound really positive. That's good. That's real good." Jackson wanted to ask her about the picture on the wall. The one taken of her sister right before she had disappeared from his life; but he couldn't see an easy way to broach the subject.

According to his calculations, Tori would have been not quite sixteen when Emily was born. Michelle's mother had been all about appearances. *Had she taken the girls and moved when Tori became pregnant at such a young age?*

He tried to remember Michelle's younger sister, but the only image that came to mind was that of a scrawny little girl, who was way too quiet and always had a book in her hands. He'd only ever spoken to her once, and that was barely memorable.

They'd all gone to the same school, but she hadn't hung out with the cheerleaders or the popular crowd, and their paths had never crossed. *Michelle! After all these years, I finally find you, but you're dead! No wonder I could not find you all those years ago!*

"Well, I'm going to let you rest. I'll take this back where I found it, shall I?" Jackson asked, picking up the oxygen bottle and heading back to the bedroom before she could answer.

When he came back out, Tori was standing on her own and looked much stronger, "I know you are probably sick of hearing doctors tell you what to do, but you really do need to take it easy and get some rest."

"Yes, sir. I plan on it."

"Sir? Really?" Jackson asked, amused that she was trying to come off all professional on him. "Jackson is fine. Tell Grace I'll stop by and introduce myself at a later time."

Jackson gave her one more appraising look and then headed out the way they first entered the backyard. Through the side gate. Moments later the growl of the Mustang's engine moved away from the house and Tori sighed in relief.

Chapter 13

Grace was beside herself with worry when she arrived home and heard the girls recount the evening's adventure. Tori tried to downplay the entire incident, but Emily and Dani were in drama mode and loving it.

"He helped momma breathe too," Emily offered.

Michael and Grace exchanged a look of concern, "How did he do that?"

"He got that green tank thing from the bedroom and put the mask over her mouth. Momma, why was your mouth that blue color? Did you have some candy?"

Michael narrowed his eyes at Tori and then shooed the girls back out into the living room. "Tori, why didn't you tell us you were having trouble breathing?"

"Because I'm not. Well, I'm not if I don't try to walk across the front yards. I just over did it, but everything turned out okay. I'm safe. The girls are safe. And Grace has her momma's wedding dress."

Grace bent down and hugged her. "You need to stop overdoing it if you ever want to fully recover."

"Yes, mom."

"And don't you forget it." Grace smiled at her and took Michael by the arm, pulling him from the room. After collecting Dani and all of her princess paraphernalia, they headed home and put her to bed.

Michael kissed Grace on the lips at the front door, "So are you excited to see your mom's dress?"

"I am. Sara is sure it will fit with only a few minor alterations. I hope she's right."

"Well, I'm going to wish you sweet dreams and get out of here so you can go play dress up. Happy Valentine's Day!" Michael kissed her tenderly, hugging her close as their lips separated and she lifted her closed eyes. "I love you, Grace."

"I love you too, Michael. More than I ever thought possible. Happy Valentine's Day!"

.. ✿ ..

"SO, MRS. HARDING, DID you enjoy your Valentine's Day surprise?" Trent asked as he helped Sara pull off her boots.

"Trent, the carriage ride was very romantic. How could I not like it?" Sara told him, kissing him on the cheek and then shivering. "You're cold!"

"So are you. Let's go warm up by the fire. It won't take but a minute to get going."

Sara nodded and then made a beeline for the couch and the blankets, "I can't feel my nose."

Trent looked her over and assured her, "Well, it's still there. A little red perhaps, but rest assured, you still have a very cute nose on your face."

Sara blushed and then giggled. She'd been waiting all day to tell him her news, but was still undecided on how to do it. When he joined her on the couch a few minutes later, and pulled her up against his chest, she forgot about it momentarily as she basked in being held close against her husband's chest. "I love you," she murmured to him.

"I love you right back. I can't believe it's been less than two months since you drove into Castle Peaks and into my life."

"So much has happened in that two months, it sometimes seems like a lifetime."

They grew quiet, wrapped in each other's arms and thoughts of what their lives had been like before each other. Trent had been content to navigate life as a bachelor, immune to the various single women the matchmaking mommas of the town had offered up.

Sara, had found herself married, and a few hours later, had been running for her life. Literally. She had ended up in his town, a few days before Christmas. Sick. Scared. And wanted by the authorities.

Trent thought about the phone call he'd received earlier that day, and then pushed it aside. There wasn't anything that could be done about the situation tonight, and he really didn't want their first Valentine's Day to be marred by the ugliness of the past.

Tipping her chin up, he kissed her softly and asked, "Ready for bed?"

Sara sighed and relaxed into his kiss, "Just about."

When Trent raised an eyebrow at her in question, she began toying with the buttons on his shirt. A dead giveaway that something was on her mind. Deciding to cut right to the chase, he asked, "What's up?"

Sara gave him a soft smile and then leaned up and whispered in his ear. She watched as his eyes got as big as saucers before a huge grin covered his face. "Really? You're sure?"

When she nodded, he kissed her and then let out a holler, "I'm gonna be a daddy!"

Sara watched him, laughing at how happy he seemed. They'd talked about trying to have a baby a few weeks ago, and she'd never dreamed they would get lucky this quickly. But they had. She was going to have a baby, sometime between Halloween and Thanksgiving.

"That's the best Valentine's gift you could have given me." Trent kissed her deeply once again and then asked, "Now, are you ready for bed?"

Sara nodded at him shyly and then giggled as he picked her up and carried her down the hallway. He was always picking her up, and she figured she might get used to the sensation in fifty years or so.

Chapter 14

Samuel waited until Jane had entered Grace's house and turned off the porch light. They had gone back to his beach house after sharing dinner with Grace and Michael. They were flying back to Castle Peaks in a few short weeks to get married and as their wedding date approached, Jane and he were finding more things that needed their attention.

The pair had decided to live in Samuel's beach house. There were several extra bedrooms, and even though they were both nearing their forties, they both were looking forward to raising a family.

Samuel turned onto the highway, planning to head home when his phone buzzed. Glancing at the screen, he immediately pulled over to the side of the road and pushed the button to connect the call.

"Trent?"

"Samuel. Are you in a place where you can talk for a few minutes?"

"Yeah. I just dropped Jane back off at Grace's house. It's got to be almost 1 o'clock in the morning. Why are you calling so late?"

"Have you checked your email today?" Trent asked in a quiet voice.

"No. I was only in the office for a few minutes earlier this morning. What's going on?"

"A buddy of mine from Virginia passed along some intel they captured over a social media site. It seems that Julian's lawyer has been talking to a couple of freelancers."

"Hit men? What is James Sewell doing talking with hit men?" Samuel asked, scratching his head in frustration. *Way to destroy a perfectly nice evening!*

"Julian's lawyer was recorded on tape, interviewing potential men, but that's not what grabbed everyone's attention. He arranged to meet with Raven."

"What?!" Samuel tried to calm his voice down, but this was *not* good news.

The Raven was a female assassin that had been operating between North and South America for the last ten years. It was believed that she alone was responsible for the recent assassination attempt on the newly elected President of Colombia. The man had promised to destroy and dismantle the drug cartels, and they were pushing back. Hard.

The Raven had been in the Top Ten Most Wanted Persons for more months than Samuel could remember, but where a recent picture normally was placed; there was nothing but a silhouette. No one knew what the Raven looked like. No one.

They knew she was female because of DNA evidence that had been collected from her victims, but that was all they knew.

"When and where is the meeting?" Samuel asked, already seeing the huge break just getting a visual on her would be for many agencies.

"James agreed to meet with her at LAX in three days' time."

"Great! That's like looking for a needle in a haystack!"

"My buddy seems to think they have a way to at least get a visual on her. It seems that James just hired a new driver. His old one was deported back to Colombia after being stopped one too many times for exceeding the speed limit."

Samuel grinned, "Let me guess. Your buddy is the new driver?"

"Got it in one. Anyway, James is going to LAX three days from now and the driver had to submit security clearance paperwork for the vehicle. They're going to the private airfield."

"I can definitely work with that. Did you send me the info on your buddy?"

"It's all in the email. Oops, Sara's awake. I don't want the women to know what's going on until they have to."

"Agreed. Give her my best and I'll call you tomorrow once I have a chance to set some things in motion." Samuel disconnected the call and then headed home.

Once there, he read the email and then sent a few of his own out. He wouldn't get any responses until the next morning, but at least things had been set in motion. If they could get visual evidence of Julian's lawyer meeting with a known assassin, the entire situation with Trevor and Julian would change. And if he and his team could get a visual on Raven, the entire world would benefit.

. . ⚘ . .

EARLY THE NEXT MORNING, Samuel and Stan met with the other members of their FBI unit to discuss the various options open to them. The LA office had designated several agents to work things from their end, and currently they were all sitting around conference tables in both locations, trying to come up with a workable plan.

The LA office had several undercover agents working at the airport, but no one in the private plane area.

The buddy Trent had mentioned had sent Samuel a brief phone picture, showing the license plate of the limo James Sewell would be arriving in. He'd also warned them against trying to place a tracker on the vehicle. It seemed that Mr. Sewell took his personal security very seriously and had anti-tracking devices everywhere he went.

"So, how do we get access to the flights that are cleared to land on the private runways?" Samuel asked, wishing he knew of someone in the FAA who owed him a favor or two. Dealing with the FAA was like dealing with the bureaucrats in D.C. – it was all around better to go over and under them and beg forgiveness afterwards.

"Flights only have to be filed twenty-four hours before their expected arrival. That protocol doesn't change just because it's a private jet rather than a commercial airliner."

"But how do we gain access to those records? Anyone brave enough to visit the tower and ask for them?"

There were chuckles around the room, on both sides of the video feed. Stan finally came up with a workable solution, "What about if we move people into the security booth and then a fuel truck. Until we get confirmation of which hangar the plane's going to, that would at least get our people on the ground and with the possibility of visuals."

"That should work," Samuel added, "the objective here is not a snatch and grab, but intel. We can't protect against that which we can't identify."

All heads nodded in agreement. "So we have two days to put this into motion. Samuel and I will coordinate on this end. We need eyes on the limo all the way."

Agent Salazar, from the LA office, spoke up, "We have enough cameras on the highway, and we should have no problem tracking the car up and back."

"Okay, Stan will coordinate on the radio on this end and we'll have cars stationed between here and there. I want to know the minute that limo leaves Sewell's home and every place it goes between now and then."

"I'm already on it. I sent a car over there this morning. Anyone have any other questions?" Samuel asked before adjourning the meeting.

When no one said anything, he disconnected the video feed and then looked at Stan and the others sitting around the office. "I want eyes on Grace and Dani until this is over."

"What about Sara?" Stan asked.

"Trent's watching Sara. As far as we know, Trevor and Julian don't know where she's at. All of the official communication between her and the FBI and Justice Department has been through the Denver office."

"Good, that's one less thing to worry about. I want access to the audio tapes of Julian and Trevor's visits with their attorney."

"Sam, you know the judge isn't going to give us access to those. Not without a heck of a good reason, which we don't have right now."

Samuel nodded his head, "Let's hope they don't give us one. I'm ready for this case to be over." His coworkers all agreed that Julian Quintana and Trevor Ward needed to be locked up and the key thrown away.

Samuel glanced at the clock, alarmed to see the entire morning was already gone. "Gotta go pick up Jane. Stan, I'll have my cell on. Let me know if anything else rears its ugly head."

"No problem. Get outta here."

Chapter 15

S amuel arrived at Jane's new kitchen just in time to be the taste tester for the new dessert menu. She had selected three chefs from the teaching kitchen at The Inferno to assist her in creating the menu that would be served at all the Top Chef restaurants nationwide. Chef Scaltini and Chef Perez were world-renowned chefs who had opened the restaurant chain six years prior, but the menu choices had gotten only mediocre reviews.

After meeting Jane, they had handed her the keys to their kitchen and asked her to design a complete menu that would provide their customers with a home-cooked meal, with a touch of refinement, at a reasonable price.

The three chefs had been given the task of coming up with two desserts each. Today was all about baking, and as each chef dished up their creation, Jane joined Samuel, bringing with her two tall glasses of ice water.

"Sure you're up for this?" she asked, noticing that he looked stressed out.

Samuel gave her a smile, "How exactly does one prepare for a dessert tasting?"

Jane laughed, "By not eating more than a bite of each. Remember, I need you to rate the dishes from best to worst."

"Worst dessert? Surely you jest," Samuel placed his hand over his heart. The man had a definite sweet tooth, something that Jane was very happy to oblige. She loved to bake.

"Chef, may I serve?" the little female chef asked, having a tray bearing two covered dishes on it.

"Thank you. Yes, you may."

The young woman placed a tray in front of Samuel and then one in front of Jane and then with a nod of her head, vacated the small dining area.

Removing the tray, Samuel was intrigued to see ten, bite-size servings of nine different baked goods. Some of them he was familiar with, but others he was not. A single serving of a bread product had been placed in the center of the tray, and there were three other breads that looked very similar, yet very different.

"Okay, first, try the bread. I want you to eat each piece and then drink some water before moving on to the next. Describe the taste, the texture, and then tell me if you like it better than the one before it."

Jane smiled at Samuel, but then stopped him when he reached for the bite of bread sitting in the middle of the tray. "Eat that one last. I'll explain why in a few minutes."

Samuel shook his head at her and then picked up a piece of bread and ate it. "This is banana bread. Not bad, but it's missing something. And it's dry." He reached for the next piece, only to have Jane point to his water glass.

He obediently drank some water before trying the second piece, "This one's much better, but the banana flavoring is almost overwhelming. And the coloring is off. Did they put food coloring in the bread?" Samuel didn't even finish the bite. Instead, he placed the rest of the piece back on the plate and then drank some more water.

"Okay, let's see if this one is any better." He took the bite and then shook his head, too much cinnamon. It's all I can taste. And the pieces of nut are too big."

Jane dutifully recorded his comments before asking, "So, out of those three, which one gets your vote?"

"Well, none of them really ring my bell. My mom makes better banana bread, and she rarely cooks anything."

Jane smiled at that and then nodded towards his plate, "Okay, now you can try the middle one."

Samuel picked up the moist bread, smelling it before popping the entire piece into his mouth. Nodding his head with a smile upon his face, he swallowed before saying, "That was amazing! Nothing like the other three samples. That one definitely gets my vote."

Jane hid her smirk and then recorded his answer. Pushing a button, she called the three chefs back into the small dining room. "Samuel has tasted all of the banana bread and has made a few comments I'd like to read back to you."

Jane read his comments back, without identifying which bread they were in reference to. Samuel watched the chefs and could tell they knew exactly which comments had been directed at their creation.

"So, Chef, which bread did he choose?" all three chefs inquired.

"Mine. Do you remember the first day we worked together and I gave you all a recipe that I wanted you to follow, exactly as it was written?"

All three heads bobbed affirmatively, and she smiled at them. "Well, every one of you looked at the recipe and found something wrong with it. A reason why the recipe needed to be changed or altered.

"This exercise was to teach you that just because something doesn't fit in the mold of something you already know, doesn't mean it doesn't work. I want you to take risks as we develop the menu, and sometimes that means going against everything you were taught about how to correctly do something."

"Yes, Chef," three voices called out in unison.

Jane smiled at all of them, pleased to see that she had gotten her point across. "Now, my recipe is sitting on the corkboard and I would love to see you all work together to develop it into something that each restaurant could use on a daily basis."

"Yes, Chef," came the reply once again and the three adults disappeared back into the kitchen.

Hands clapping drew her and Samuel's attention to the shadows behind them. When Chef Marco Scaltini stepped out, Jane felt herself blushing and hoped she hadn't overstepped her bounds.

"Chef, I didn't know you were going to stop by today," Jane informed him, standing and kissing the man on both cheeks.

He returned the greeting and then shook Samuel's hand. "It looks like I arrived just in time. You handled those three beautifully. Congratulations."

Jane blushed and Samuel thought it was the cutest thing he'd seen in a long time. She had appeared so confident when dealing with the three people working for her, but when faced with the famous chef, her self-confidence flew out the window. Samuel was intent on fixing that. Right now.

""Chef, have you had the privilege of tasting Jane's banana bread?"

"No, I can't say that I have. After that demonstration, I look forward to it."

Samuel nodded and then offered Jane's tray to the man, "It's the piece in the middle."

Marco picked the bite of banana bread off of the tray. He observed the texture and aroma of the bread, before placing it in his mouth and then closing his eyes in pleasure. "Oh, this is good. This is really good! Jane, you are a cooking genius!"

Jane blushed more and then ducked her head. "Thank you, but I'm sure you could create something just as good."

Marco shook his head, "No, actually I cannot. Baking was never my thing. I did try, but my soufflés all fell, my cakes burned on the edges, and my breads were always doughy in the middle."

"Is that true?" Jane asked in amazement.

"Very. Ask Perez when you see her next. There is a reason she teaches the baking and dessert classes. Now, tell me what is in this bread and where the remainder of the loaf is."

Jane laughed and promptly retrieved the rest of the loaf, cutting Samuel and Marco both a large slice. "Ingredients please," Marco reminded her, slathering his slice with soft butter.

"The usual things: flour, sugar, eggs, butter, salt, baking soda, and milk."

"I wasn't asking for the usual things. What else is in here?"

"Well, I use cinnamon and vanilla, of course. And the riper the bananas, the better I think it tastes. But the secret ingredient is the vanilla pudding mix."

"Pudding mix? In bread?"

"Yep. It keeps it moist and helps bring out the flavor."

"Why vanilla? Why not banana pudding?"

Jane shook her head, "I did try that one time, but it was too much flavor."

"Well, whatever and however you make this, I want it on the menu. A plate full of that macaroni and cheese you cooked for us several weeks ago, and this for dessert and I'd never eat anywhere else."

"Thank you for your kind words."

"Not kind. Honest. There is a difference."

Chapter 16

Jackson woke the next morning still unable to think of anything but the woman he'd met the night before. *Tori. Michelle's sister?*

He started packing up his library, only to grow frustrated a few hours later. He couldn't concentrate on anything except those pictures.

Jumping back in his car, he made the ten minute drive back to Tori's house and parked in her driveway. Glancing at his watch, he realized it was already 12:30 p.m. and he hoped she'd gotten some much needed sleep the night before.

She'd seemed confident in her ability to assess her situation because she was a nurse, but Jackson had seen the dark circles beneath her eyes and felt the frailness of her body as he'd helped her back to her house. She might have finished her chemo, but she was by no means out of the woods. Now her body had to strengthen itself and heal!

He sat in his car for five minutes before he finally got up the nerve to go knock on the door. He'd thought he had the past locked away. Sure, Sara had dragged some of it up, but he'd firmly put it back in place again. Now it was coming to the forefront, but in the form of real life people. Not so easy to put away when confronted with living, breathing memories.

Climbing from his car, he walked around the hood of the car and then he had a sudden image of himself driving a truck. Mentally smacking his head, he stopped and looked at his beautiful Mustang. He loved that car! But it was completely impractical for where he was moving. No! He needed a truck, or a SUV of some sort. Something with four wheel drive and plenty of space would be ideal.

Adding that to his to-do list, he sighed and then finished the walk to the front door, surprised to see the inner door open and Tori standing there watching him.

"Hey!" he told her with a crooked smile as he drew close to the screen door.

"Why are you here?" Tori asked without prevarication. She knew she was blushing at the complete fool she'd made of herself the night before. She'd gone against everything she'd always told her patients and pushed too hard too fast. She'd suffered the consequences as well.

"I wanted to make sure you were doing okay," Jackson said, and then added, "I was in the area and thought I'd just swing by."

"You were in the area?" Tori asked, narrowing her eyes at him in disbelief.

"Well, yeah! After I turned into this subdivision, I was definitely in the area." Jackson smiled when she gave a short laugh at his humor. "Can I come in for a few minutes?"

Tori backed away from the door. "Suit yourself. I have puppies to feed."

Tori turned and slowly made her way to the kitchen and out onto the back patio. The puppies immediately got excited with most either licking her feet or jumping up at her legs and begging for attention. Shelby, was lying in the shade of the big tree and only lifted her head as Tori began a one-sided conversation with the pups.

"Who's hungry? I have puppy chow wet, or puppy chow dry." She poured dry food into the two bowls, wetting one of them and giving it a brief stir with the wooden spoon left on the patio for just that occasion. When she set the bowls on the concrete, the puppies pushed and shoved each other, trying to get around the bowls.

Some of them tried the wet food, only to immediately switch bowls, opting for the crunchy dry morsels. Others did the opposite. Before long, each puppy had located its personal preference and was eating happily. Tori watched for a few minutes and then a movement at the backdoor snagged her attention.

Jackson stood there watching her and the pups, "They're good eaters." He didn't know what else to say, and having looked at the pictures again, he knew he couldn't leave without knowing the entire story of what had happened his senior year.

"Yeah." Tori grabbed a can of dog food, opened it and dumped it into a smaller stainless steel bowl and then carried it to the opposite side of the patio. "Shelby, come on girl. Time to eat while you can."

Shelby brushed up against Tori's legs as she stopped to get petted and then quickly devoured her food before the puppies were finished. Tori sat down in one of the patio chairs, needing a small break before she headed inside to tackle the mound of laundry that had begun to pile up. Grace and Jane had both offered to handle the task, but Tori had adamantly denied needing help to manage her household chores. She'd done it throughout her illness, and now that she was cured, there was no reason she couldn't continue to do so. It might take her a little longer this week, but she'd get her chores done.

"So, satisfied that I'm better than yesterday?" Tori asked, eyeing the man who was seating himself next to her. She still couldn't get over the niggling feeling that she knew him from somewhere.

"You seem to have a little more energy today," Jackson commented, watching her and not commenting on the fact that she wasn't wearing that blonde wig today. Her hair looked like it had begun to grow back, but if she'd just finished another round of chemo, what little growth there was would soon fall out once again.

Tori leaned her head back against the chair and that's when she must have realized she didn't have the wig on. Jackson watched as her eyes popped back open and a blush quickly rose to cover her entire face and scalp. When she hesitantly raised a hand to her head, wanting verification of what she already knew to be true, he rushed to assure her it didn't matter to him.

"Tori, don't let it worry you." Jackson watched as she looked at him with shame and humiliation burning in her face and he wondered at the cause. *Had someone made her feel badly about herself because she'd gotten sick and the cure had made her hair fall out? They should be shot!* He realized he was furious on her behalf and while she struggled with her embarrassment, he struggled with his anger.

"Who was it?" he asked in a quiet voice.

Tori could hear the anger in his voice and found herself puzzled by it. This man didn't even know her, yet he was angry, and it didn't appear to be at her, but her circumstances.

"Who was what?"

"Who taught you to be embarrassed because you got sick?"

Tori gasped and ducked her head. Swallowing, she struggled to push the hateful words that rushed to the surface back where they belonged. In the grave. They'd never actually been said to her. Just in her head.

"Tori, it's not your fault you got sick. You know that, right?"

Tori nodded, "Of course I know that. I worked on the oncology floor, remember? I can't tell you how many times I had this same conversation with a patient. What I don't understand is why you think you need to have it with me?"

Jackson watched her and then softly said, "Because you are sitting there, embarrassed and wanting nothing more than to rush back inside the house and lock the door. Tell me I'm wrong?"

Tori looked at him for several long moments, before finally shaking her head, "I can't. And before you go psychoanalyzing me, I know in my mind that getting sick wasn't my fault. But you didn't grow up listening to your mother criticize every little aspect of your life. Or with the knowledge that whatever you did was never going to be good enough to appease her."

"No, I didn't grow up that way. My parents were wonderful and very supportive of my siblings and me."

"Lucky you," Tori threw out before she could stop herself. She wasn't jealous, just matter of fact. She did think people who'd grown up with a support structure around them were lucky. The fact that she'd never known that was also a fact. One that unfortunately seemed to govern how she made her decisions and thought about herself far too often.

"Why are you really here?" Tori asked, sensing that he wanted to ask her something. Her energy was starting to flag and she only had a few more hours before Emily would be walking in the door. She needed to accomplish something worthwhile today. She had to!

"Those pictures in your living room," Jackson began and then stopped. *How was he to go about this?* "Tell me about your family."

Tori looked at him and then back towards the house before asking, "Why? They're just pictures."

Jackson shook his head, "No, they're memories."

"Yes, but they're my memories and most of them aren't at all happy."

"Tell me."

Tori was again puzzled and queried, "Why? Why do you want me to tell you about people from my past that have been dead for a while now?"

Jackson was quiet for the longest time as he struggled with how much to reveal. Deciding to go for broke, he quietly looked at her and murmured,

"Because I knew your sister. I was planning on marrying her before that woman who called herself your mother stole her away in the middle of the night."

Tori gasped and clutched her chest. *That's where she knew him from! Oregon! Jackson was JD! The starting point guard for the basketball team and her sister's boyfriend! And that made him...* She watched him and then a new horror began to take shape in her mind and she pushed herself from the chair, headed for the house. "You need to leave. Now!" *He has to leave; I can't let him stay here. Can't let him know the truth!*

Jackson was intrigued by her response to his statement that he'd known her sister. She was in a full-blown panic, and he was at a loss to understand why. "Tori?" he asked, following her back into the house where she made a point of going to the front door and standing by it.

"Please, just leave."

Jackson could hear the emotion in her voice and knew he couldn't leave her upset like this. "Look, I don't know what's going on around here, but I'm not leaving without some answers. Why don't we sit down and talk for a few minutes?"

Tori shook her head, "I have things to do. Please..."

Jackson reached out to her, touching her on the arm, shocked at the tingling sensation that contact created. When Tori pulled her arm away from his touch and wrapped it around herself, he realized he needed to assure her he was safe and didn't mean her any harm.

"What kind of things do you need to do?" he asked, trying to put her at ease.

"Things. Chores."

"Dishes? Laundry? Vacuuming? I could stick around and help while we talk."

Tori looked at him and laughed, "You're offering to help me clean the house so that I'll talk to you about my dead sister and mother?"

"Yeah, I am."

"Why do you want to talk about them?"

Jackson was silent for a moment and then told her, "Because when your sister disappeared, it changed my life. Irrevocably. I looked for her for months afterwards."

That statement brought Tori's head up and she saw him for the first time; really saw him. She looked into his green eyes and what she saw there had her caving in. *He needs closure!*

"Fine. Are you any good at laundry? If I don't get a few loads done, Grace and Jane are going to take over and do it for me."

"And that would be horrible, why?" Jackson asked, following her slow progress to the laundry room.

"I've managed to take care of myself and Emily for all of these months, I can do so now. I'm cured and I need to get on with my life."

Jackson watched her start loading towels into the washer, gently pushing her out of the way after seeing what her intent was. When he had all of the towels loaded, he added detergent and fabric softener to the machine and then turned to ask, "What's next?"

"You're really going to stick around and help me clean the house?" Tori asked, watching him with a bemused look upon her face.

"Sure. But first, you are going to take a break and get your breathing back under control."

Tori opened her mouth to answer, but then sighed and nodded resignedly. Trudging back to the living room, she lowered herself onto the couch and relaxed into the cushions. *I really need a nap!*

"So, you dated my sister in high school, huh?" Tori mused. "I knew she was dating some basketball star, but I think I only saw you with her once. We didn't exactly hang out with the same crowds."

Jackson seated himself on the couch and nodded, "I vaguely remember you opening the door to me once or twice. I was shocked because I didn't even know she had a sister until that moment. You were a grade behind her?"

"Two. I was a sophomore when we left Oregon."

"Where did you go?" Jackson asked, not ready to ask the 'why' yet.

"To here." Tori let the silence simmer for a moment before she said, "Why don't you ask what you really want to know?"

"Fine. Why did your mother pack you all up and leave town in the middle of the night?"

Tori laughed, knowing it would have come to this sooner or later. Might as well be sooner. "Because she was embarrassed. With a baby on the way, she couldn't face her friends in town. My mother didn't like being embarrassed by her children, so rather than staying, we moved. To a new town. To someplace where there were so many people, no one even glanced twice at a pregnant teenager."

Jackson was stunned, "You mother wasn't a very nice person, was she?"

Tori gave a half-laugh, half-snort, "My mother was the most selfish, narcissistic person on the planet. She cared about nothing but herself, and that her daughters didn't embarrass her or draw attention to themselves. I tried to become a shadow, the less I was seen or heard from the better off I was. Michelle on the other hand flaunted her beauty, always wanting to be in the spotlight. My mother couldn't stand it."

"You said yesterday that they died around the time Emily was born. What happened?"

Chapter 17

"We were hit by a driver trying to elude the police; a high-speed chase that ended when the driver slammed into our car on the highway, going over a hundred miles an hour. By the time my mother saw him coming towards us, there was no time to get out of his way.

"My mother was killed instantly, but Michelle lived for a few hours, and I suffered only minor cuts and bruises. Emily was born, Michelle died, and I was left to pick up the pieces."

Jackson looked at her and quietly told her, "You fought back and won. How old were you?"

"Sixteen. I'd just turned sixteen the week before this all happened."

Sixteen! "Did they catch the driver?"

"Yeah. He died at the scene. The newspaper said he was drunk and had illegal drugs in his system, but I don't remember much else. Emily was born a few weeks early so they kept her in the hospital. When they released her, I brought her home.

"My mom had a small life insurance policy that paid for this house and my nursing degree with some to spare for Emily in the future. We've made it work." Tori watched him, waiting for him to ask her who the father was. When he didn't, she was unsure of how to proceed.

"Thank you for telling me what happened. After all of these years, it helps." *Michelle was forced to leave me. She might have been cheating on me, but she hadn't left me willingly.* Why that made a difference, Jackson couldn't say. Somehow, knowing that she hadn't been the one to leave, made her defection and unfaithfulness less damaging.

"So, what's next on your chore list?"

"A nap," came out of Tori's mouth before she could stop it. Covering her face with a hand, she tried to find a way to take back the statement, but Jackson had definitely heard it.

"That sounds like the most intelligent thing you've said. Have you had lunch yet?" he asked, making his way into her kitchen as if he did it all the time.

Tori slowly followed him, "Yeah, I had some soup earlier."

"Good. Now, off to bed with you. I'll take care of the dishes while you rest."

"Don't you have other things to do?"

Jackson smiled at her and she was amazed at how handsome he was, "Nope. I am at loose ends for the next few weeks. I'm moving up to Montana, and short of packing up all of my worldly possessions, I have nothing to do at all."

Tori yawned, unable to stop it, and saw him hide a smile. "I shouldn't be this tired," she murmured to herself.

"I heard that." Jackson watched her and then asked, "When did you have blood work done last?"

"Oh, please don't play doctor right now! I'm so tired of being poked and prodded and having my every breath watched as if it was going to be my last. I'm cancer free. My body has been pumped full of chemicals for the last time. I just want to be normal again." Tori didn't realize she'd started to cry until Jackson pulled her against his chest and rubbed her back.

"It's alright. You've done a remarkable job so far, you just need a little help to get over this last setback. I only asked because it's what I do. I can't help it."

Tori sighed and then pushed away from his chest. His very strong, warm chest. *I didn't realize being held could feel so good!* "I'm sorry. My reaction was a little over the top, even for me. I know you're only doing what any good doctor would do. Trying to find a reason for the symptoms and treat it." Tori was silent and then offered, "They drew blood when I was in the office a couple of weeks ago. I was supposed to go back last week, but then I started coughing and they just prescribed some antibiotics over the phone and told me to come back in when I felt stronger."

"Why didn't they send someone out to draw your blood?" Jackson watched her and then answered it himself, "Because you told them you were capable of coming to the hospital."

Tori nodded tiredly, "I am. Just not today."

"Or yesterday, or the day before that..."

"I'm getting stronger each day. I really am. You should have seen me the first time I met Grace and Jane. It was the day after my last chemo and I was so sick. I'm surprised they didn't just call the ambulance and make me deal with it. But they didn't. They stuck around, starting helping me take care of Emily. That was only a few weeks ago, but it seems like months."

Jackson took her elbow and led her towards the bedroom where he'd found the oxygen bottle the day before. "Take a nap. I'm sure I can find plenty of things to do around here. I'll be here when you wake up and we'll talk some more. I really think you need to have your blood work done and I would be happy to drive you to the hospital myself."

"We'll see. Jackson, you don't have to stick around. Emily knows how to get in the house and will wake me up when she gets home."

Jackson nodded his head, "Okay. I'll take care of the dishes in the sink first. I'll leave my number by the phone."

"Thanks," Tori told him, opening the door to the bedroom, and eyeing the bed with longing. *I just need a small nap and then I'll finish the laundry. It was nice of Jackson to offer to stick around, but I've been doing things by myself for a while now. I can handle it.*

• • ☙ • •

TORI SLEPT SOUNDLY, stretching and then glancing at the clock before sitting up in the bed, alarm bells going off in her head. *Where was Emily and why hadn't she awakened her? It's 6 o'clock. She should have been home hours ago!*

Tori stumbled from the bedroom, her thin tank top and sweatpants forgotten as she searched for her missing child. "Emily?! Emily?!"

"Momma, what's wrong?" came the tearful reply as Emily came barreling in from the backyard.

Tori grabbed her, hugging her close, "You didn't wake me up. I thought something had happened to you."

"Jackson said to let you sleep," Emily told her, hugging her close.

"Jackson was still here when you got home?" Tori asked, still holding onto the little girl, not only to calm her fears, but because the room was spinning and she was afraid of falling down if she let go.

"Momma, you're squeezing me really tight," Emily complained as she tried to extricate herself from the hug.

"Emmy, momma needs to go sit down on the couch. Can you help me before you go back outside?"

"I've got her, sweetie," Jackson said, moving Emily away from her mother at the same time he bent and picked her up in his arms.

Tori squeaked in surprise and then looked up into his strong face, "Why are you still here?"

"Because you still need help. Couch you said?"

"I can walk."

"No you can't." Jackson leaned down and whispered in her ear, "You might be able to fool Emily, but you were seconds from crashing to the floor. I could see it on your face, so stop trying to pretend otherwise."

Tori sagged against his chest in defeat, "Fine. Yes, the couch would be lovely." *Before I start liking being held in your arms too much!*

"Now, Grace said she and Michael would be over around 6:30 p.m. with a couple of pizzas, to which Emily and Dani screamed in delight, scaring the puppies in the process. I've switched out the laundry a few times, the dishes are done, and..." Jackson leaned over to look her in the eyes, "I dusted and swept the carpets."

He sat her down on the couch and then pulled a blanket over her lap. When he stood up, he got his first good look at her and tried not to cringe at what he saw. Her skin tone was very pale, almost translucent in places it was so white, but it was the evidence of her cancer that had caught his attention.

They hadn't discussed what type of cancer she'd had, but now it was obvious. *Breast cancer!* The thin tank top she wore, didn't conceal the scarring or healing skin that was evident beneath the white fabric. Pulling her blanket up over her shoulders, he tried to focus on something else, not wanting to embarrass her or himself.

"Emily helped me fold the towels and put them away. I think she must have corrected me ten times about folding them the wrong way," he said, trying for anything that might ease the tension that had suddenly filled the room.

Tori knew exactly what had happened. She'd seen his eyes fixed on her chest and knew without even looking down what he would have seen. Her tank top was thin; having been washed so many times the fabric was almost washed away. She knew he would have seen the deformity and disfigurement caused by the removal of her breast, as well as the shadow of the healing incisions.

She watched his reaction and when he deftly changed the subject, she was both relieved and hurt. The counselors at the hospital had tried to help her deal with what she viewed as the loss of her femininity. Her doctor had already started talking to her about reconstructive surgery, and now that her chemo was completed, that was the logical conclusion.

After the surgery, she would look just like she had before. Only she would know the true toll the cancer had taken on her body. *Only one functioning breast. The inability to have children.* The list was probably longer, but those things were the only ones that mattered to her.

Pulling the blanket up under her chin, she dropped her head and struggled not to let his reaction matter. *So what if he didn't think her attractive! It wasn't like she hadn't spent the last nine years doing without a man around. She didn't need a man to define her. She had Emily and that would be enough. It had to be!*

Jackson watched the emotions flow over Tori's face and knew he hadn't covered his reaction very well. Sitting down on the edge of the couch, he gently tipped her face up to meet his eyes, "Tori, I'm sorry. I didn't know. You told me you had cancer, but not what kind."

Tori shook her head, looking away from him, "It doesn't matter. Really. I should have put my sweatshirt back on."

"Tori, you can't hide what happened."

"Oh yeah? Watch me. And why does any of this matter to you? Before yesterday, you didn't even know I existed. Well, I mean... I guess you knew I existed, but you didn't know anything about me."

"Stop being so defensive! You are an amazing woman and a survivor. Stop feeling sorry for yourself!"

"Um...if I'm interrupting something, I can always come back later," a small voice said, drawing both their attention to the front door.

Jackson had called her doctor who had readily agreed to send a nurse over to draw her blood. Jackson suspected that the last round of chemo had left her anemic, but without bloodwork to back it up, the problem couldn't be adequately treated. "No, no problem. Come on in."

Jackson stood up, prepared to battle with her over this decision. When all she did was give him a look, he hid a smile and then moved back to allow the little nurse to work.

"Hey, Tori. Doc said you weren't feeling too hot." She proceeded to tell Tori which tests had been ordered and promised the results would be ready later on in the evening. It seemed everyone at the hospital knew Tori and were willing to go out of their way to help her, if she would simply let them.

"Thanks, Stacie. I didn't mean to put you out..."

"Girl, would you shut up! We've all been trying to help you for months now. I'm glad to see someone finally took charge and is helping you regardless. You can't get better if you keep running yourself down. You know that!" she offered as she packed up her supplies.

"Yeah, yeah. I do. But once you're on this side of the bed, then we'll talk. I'd much rather be the nurse than the patient."

"Wouldn't we all. Hey, I'll run these back to the lab. Take care of you and that little one."

"I will, Stacie. Thanks."

"No problem. Nice to meet you," she told Jackson as she headed out the door as quickly as she'd arrived.

"Friend of yours?" he asked, preparing himself for the fireworks.

"We worked together at the hospital for a while. She got tired of that environment and went to work as my oncologist's staff lab tech. She loves her job now."

"You sound jealous," Jackson pointed out.

"I guess maybe I am. The hospital environment is interesting, but now that I've been out of it for so many months, I'm really not looking forward to going back to it."

"So don't!"

"Just like that, huh? And where else would I use my skills? For the last five years, all I've done is work with cancer patients. Michael offered me a job at the new pediatric clinic he's opening, but I don't think I could handle working strictly with kids. In fact, I'm sure I couldn't handle it."

"Yeah, working with sick kids everyday would be hard."

"There she is," Grace called out as she entered the house carrying two pizza boxes. Michael entered behind her with a large bowl of salad and a covered container of dessert. "Did you sleep well?" Grace asked, coming over and giving Tori a hug.

Tori smiled and nodded. "I did. You guys didn't have to bring dinner over."

"No problem," Michael assured her. "I'm actually using it as an excuse to talk to Jackson here."

Grace smiled at the men and then shooed them out the door, "You boys go have your talk and watch the girls play." Once the men were out of the house, Grace turned to Tori and asked, "Feel up to a shower before dinner?"

Tori moaned in response, "Oh that sounds wonderful. How did you know?"

"Does it really matter?" she asked with a quirk of her brow.

"No. No, it doesn't." Grace helped Tori back to the bedroom and went in search of clean clothes while the woman took a shower, using the shower stool for support when she grew tired. She wasn't sure how Grace had known that was what she needed, but it had been exactly the right thing to help refocus her mind and energy.

Chapter 18

"Trent, we don't think there's any danger to Sara, but keep her close until you hear back from me," Samuel said.

"I take it you all have a plan in place?" Trent asked, motioning for Becky to shut the door to his office.

"Yeah. We're only after visual identification right now. We need to know what this woman looks like so we can track her movements. Without any sort of eyewitness evidence, we'd never come close to getting a conviction if we just arrested her for meeting with Sewell."

Trent nodded his head, "I hear you. Well, let me know if there's anything I can do from this end."

"Will do. Now, about the wedding coming up...would you stand up with me?" Samuel asked, knowing that Jane had already asked Sara to be her maid of honor.

"Man, I'd be honored. You thinking of doing the whole dress-up thing?" Trent asked, thinking he'd need to take a trip to find a tux if that was the case.

"No!" Samuel stated so quickly, Trent couldn't help but laugh.

"Got it! No tux! Definitely no tux!"

"You laugh, but when was the last time you voluntarily put yourself in one of them monkey suits?"

"Oh, come on. They're not so bad. But I'm with you. So what, suits and ties?"

"Yeah. I'm going with a brown theme to match Jane's peach dress. I haven't seen the dress yet, but she bought it here in California, so I can assure you it isn't going to offer anything in the way of keeping her warm."

Trent could hear the planning in his friend's voice and asked, "What did you have in mind?"

Samuel spent the next thirty minutes planning with Trent. When the two men hung up their phones, a plan had been devised to give Jane the romance she'd said she didn't need or want in a wedding. Sometimes, a man just had to make a decision and go with it. Samuel couldn't wait until the wedding. Jane was going to get romanced right off her feet!

. . ⚓ . .

TORI STOOD UNDER THE spray of the hot shower and tipped her head back. The warm water felt so good against her skin, and after washing her hair and rinsing it, she had to admit she lacked the energy to do more than just stand there.

After another couple of minutes, she heard Grace ask if she was ready to get out and she sighed and answered, "Yes."

Tori turned the water off and then reached for the towel. Grace had hung it over the top rail of the shower enclosure, and it took all of her energy to reach up and pull it down. She dried her face and then wiped the dry towel over her head. *Remember when you used to have enough hair you needed two towels when you took a shower?*

She let a hand lightly touch her scalp, almost crying when she felt how smooth it was. What little hair she had was falling out, thanks to the last round of chemo and now she had to start all over. *At least it was the last round! This time when your hair grows back, it might get longer than a quarter of an inch before falling out!*

Grace knocked on the door once again and then opened a crack, "Tori, are you okay in here?"

"Yeah, just feeling sorry for myself." She wrapped the towel around her and then stepped from the shower, sinking down to sit on the closed toilet lid while her energy level recovered.

"That's understandable. I brought you some clothes. Can you manage, or do you need some help?"

Tori looked up and met Grace's eyes, "I hate to admit this, but I guess I'm going to need some help. If you don't mind that is."

"Do you want me to get Emily...?"

"No! I don't want her to see me... I mean, she hasn't seen..."

Grace stepped inside the room and then closed the door, "Honey, it's okay. You don't want Emily to see your scar. It's okay. Let's get you dressed and then go eat."

"Is Jackson still here?" Tori asked as Grace helped her pull a clean tank top over her body, a darker one this time that hid her scars, but not her disfigurement. "Can you get me a sweatshirt as well?"

"Are you cold?" Grace asked in concern, sweating from the steam the shower had created. It was almost still in the high seventies outside, an uncharacteristic heat wave having moved through Southern California in the last few days.

"No, but... I can't go out there in just a tank top."

Grace looked at her and then asked, "Tori, are you planning on covering up your body for the rest of your life?" Hearing her own voice, she paused and waited for Tori to tell her to get out. *I'm butting in and it would serve me right if she told me to take a hike and mind my own business!*

"Grace, look at me. I mean, really look. I may be cancer free, but what it left behind is hideous. I can't even look like a woman right now!"

"Tori, everyone understands..."

"I don't! I know this doesn't make any sense, but I feel so violated! The cancer took so much from me, and I can't ever get it back."

"What about reconstructive surgery?" Grace asked, having already discussed this with Tori when she was in a better frame of mind. She wasn't sure what had her thinking about herself like this, but she wondered if it didn't have to do with the gorgeous man sitting in the other room.

"Yeah, it will make things look better. But that can't happen for at least the next two weeks. And then I'll have another surgery to recover from."

Grace could see the pity party was building steam and decided it was time for some tough love. "Are you listening to yourself? How many of the women you took care of didn't get the chance you have? How many of their husbands, and children can only go to a gravesite to remember them?"

"You're alive! You may not like the way things look right now, or how crummy you still feel, but you're alive! You will wake up tomorrow and have the opportunity to change the superficial things you don't like. How many other women never get that chance?" *People like my mother!*

Tori opened her mouth and then closed it. "I..."

"You know what, Tori? You are so blessed but you don't see it. Not all the time anyway. Stop letting the cancer win, and live!"

Tori released the tears that had been tightly held for so many months, sobbing even harder when Grace wrapped her arms around her and murmured, "Shush. Oh, I'm sorry. I didn't mean to attack you. Really, please quit crying."

Tori shook her head, "No! You're right. I am blessed and the longer I feel sorry for myself, the longer the cancer wins. I can't let that happen." After several minutes, she pushed away from Grace and then gave her a tremulous smile. "Thanks. For everything. You and Jane have blessed me in so many ways..."

"Don't, or we'll be crying again. Do you want one of the wigs?"

Tori blew her nose and then shook her head, "No! This is who I am right now, and if anybody has a problem with it, they can leave."

"You know that neither of those men out there are going to care, right? They've see it all, and it won't even phase them."

"I don't quite believe you, but then again, they're only doctors, not boyfriends. A boyfriend would care."

"You really believe that, don't you?"

Tori shrugged but then walked from the bathroom. She didn't look at herself in the mirror, nor did she hesitate when she opened the door and headed for the kitchen. She knew Michael wouldn't care, but he didn't look at her like a woman. As for Jackson, she didn't know him very well, and while he was gorgeous, she knew he didn't really see her as a woman either. Just another victim of a horrible disease he fought every day.

"Hey, momma, feeling better?" Michael asked as he entered the house, followed by Jackson.

"Yes, thanks." She briefly met his eyes, but didn't even acknowledge that Jackson was in the room. She couldn't. The girls entered moments later, forgetting to shut the door all the way, and before anyone knew what was happening, a flood of little puppies crashed through the doorway.

Tori watched the men struggle to capture the puppies, who were slipping on the tiled surface and crashing into one another. When Shelby came in, she decided this must be some sort of new game and started barking. Grace had entered the kitchen, and the women could do nothing but watch and laugh.

It took almost ten minutes before all of the puppies had been corralled and put back outside, along with their mother. The men were scowling when they reentered the house and Grace and Tori just laughed all that much harder. Emily was laughing, but not Dani.

Grace watched her daughter's face and tried to head off the tantrum that was brewing. "Girls, why don't you come get some dinner on your plates first?"

Emily readily agreed, but Dani stood in the middle of the room and crossed her arms over her chest. Preparing herself for battle, Grace asked, "Dani, what's wrong?"

"I wants to eat with the puppies."

"Well, the puppies have to stay outside. Why don't you come eat and then you can go back outside and play with them?"

Dani shook her head, "No! I want to eat with them."

Tori saw the storm clouds brewing in the little girls face and spoke up, "Dani, where did you want to eat?"

"Inside!" Princess Dani informed the room.

Tori shook her head, "Dani, the puppies would make a big mess if we let them in the house. They aren't housebroken."

The new word gave Dani pause, "Aunt Tori, they won't break the house. They're too little to break the house."

"No, sweetie. Housebroken means they know they have to go outside to go potty."

Dani thought about that for so long, Grace wondered what was going to come out of her daughter's mouth next. She didn't have to wait for long, "You has a bathroom cuz I's used it."

Tori nodded, "Yes, but that bathroom is only for people."

"Oh." When she looked up at Grace, she nodded her head and said, "Momma, we's got to get a doggy potty before the puppies come home. I's don't want them to potty outside and Aunt Tori said..."

"Dani, we are not going to put a doggy potty in the house." Grace needed to make that fact perfectly clear to her daughter. Right now!

Michael smirked and she turned on him, "Think this conversation is funny? It's all yours now. Let's see how well you fare against the logic of a four-year-old."

Jackson had sidled up next to Tori and whispered, "That's logic?"

Tori looked up at him, "Ever try to reason with a four-year-old?" When he shook his head, she smiled and advised him, "Don't. You'll lose every time."

Jackson watched the smile light up her face. *She needs to do that more often!* Pulling himself back from that thought, he watched as she busied herself fixing the girls plates of food. She'd forgotten the wig and then hadn't covered her body up. The black of the tank top did a good job of camouflaging her healing body, and as she joked with Grace and Michael, he picked up on a new attitude coming from her. He liked it.

After dinner was put away, Michael asked, "So did you think any more about my offer?"

Tori nodded her head, "Michael, I can't work with sick kids all day. It would be too hard. I just couldn't do it."

Michael gave her an understanding look, "I completely understand. There are days when I feel the same way, but then there are days where good things happen and they make up for it. So, what are your plans then?"

Tori shook her head, "I really don't know."

"Why not just go back to your old job?" Jackson asked.

"I can't. I was entitled to the standard twelve weeks of leave, but the hospital where I worked has new management and they were unwilling to give me more than that. The most I could hope for would be the temp pool, and then I'd have to work any shift they gave me. I can't do that to Emily."

"You shouldn't have to." Jackson was outraged. It wasn't her fault she'd gotten sick, but she was being penalized for it anyway. "So, are you wanting to stay in oncology work?"

Tori glanced at him and then away, "I think so. I don't know. I guess I might have to sell the house and move."

That thought had everyone drawing silent while they finished eating. Grace broke the tension by saying, "I wouldn't worry about it right now. These things have a way of working themselves out. Now, who wants dessert?"

Chapter 19

Grace and Michael took Dani home an hour later, and Tori sent Emily off for a quick shower. The little girl had been forced to grow up while Tori was sick and was now capable of doing a lot of things for herself.

When Jackson's phone rang, he answered it and then said, "Hang on a sec and let me put you on speakerphone so Tori can listen as well." He got her attention and then gestured for her to listen. "Okay, she's listening."

"Tori, Dr. Samuels. I was just calling to give you the results of the blood test. Everything looks fine, but you are slightly anemic just like Jackson suspected. I'm going to call in a prescription for some iron tablets and I want to check your levels again in a week. You know the other things you can do to help things along. Any questions?"

"No, thank you for calling so quickly."

"No problem, hon. How are you doing other than feeling like someone replaced your blood with water?"

Tori laughed as she realized that's exactly how she'd been feeling. Couple that with the respiratory infection and it was no wonder she had no energy. "I'm good. The antibiotics seemed to have done the trick."

"Good. Well, you have my number and I expect you to use it if you need to. On another note, any luck getting your old job back? I miss seeing you on the floor."

"No, and I don't think I could work there again, anyway. I'll find something when I'm ready."

"Did you schedule with Dr. Chevas yet?"

Tori could feel the question coming from Jackson before he even asked it, but she ignored him, "No. I think I'll do that in the morning."

"Good. I'll sign off on it as long as it's not any sooner than two weeks. You need to put this all behind you."

"I know. I'll call first thing tomorrow. Thank you."

"Be good. Jackson, you have my number. Make her call if she has any problems."

"I'll do that. Thanks for rushing that lab work through. I'll run down to the drugstore and pick up her pills so she can start them tonight."

"Fantastic! I'll call the order in right now. Goodnight!"

"You don't have to do that," Tori told him as he closed his phone and slipped it back into his pocket.

"Who is Dr. Chevas?"

Tori stared at him and then crossed her arms over her chest. The movement brought home her deformity so she uncrossed them and then turned slightly away from him, "She's a reconstructive surgeon. Don't you have some packing to do, or someplace to be?"

Jackson could see she was getting defensive and he didn't want their interaction to end up there again. "I'll go grab your pills. Which pharmacy?"

"The one down on the corner, two blocks east."

"Got it. I'll be back in a few minutes." Jackson left before he could say something else. *What is it about her? He didn't know her, had only spent a few hours with her ever, but he was finding it hard to leave her alone.*

Jackson retrieved her pills, but she met him at the front door with an unwelcoming look on her face, "Thanks. I won't keep you any longer. I hope you found the closure you were looking for. Thanks again." Tori shut the door in his face and he stood there for a few more minutes before walking back to his car.

Jackson drove home, trying to put Tori and her daughter from his mind, but just as the night before, it didn't work. The next day, he busied himself with trading off his beloved Mustang for a Toyota SUV with all the bells and whistles.

He made arrangements for the movers' to come at the end of the next week and pack up the belongings he would be moving to Montana, and then contacted a local charity store and made arrangements for them to take the rest of his furniture. He wouldn't need it where he was going and there was no reason to store it. None of it had sentimental value and he was pleased with his accomplishments when he retired for the day.

Throughout the day, his thoughts had drifted to Tori and her daughter, but he'd pushed them away. She was just a woman he'd crossed paths with and he was leaving town in less than two weeks. No, Tori and her daughter were better off left alone.

That thought worked well for him over the next two days, but then he found the small envelope Sara had asked him to give Grace still stuck in his overnight bag. He'd forgotten to leave it with the dress! Setting it aside, he made plans to deliver it the next day.

· · ⚮ · ·

SAMUEL AND STAN FOUND themselves sitting in the conference room once again, three days later pouring over surveillance tapes and watching as their video experts worked their magic. The operation at LAX had been as much of a success as was possible, given the circumstances, and they had over twenty minutes of video footage.

"We'll run this through facial recognition software and see if anything pops."

"How long will that take?" Samuel asked, feeling the clock already ticking.

"A few hours, maybe a few days. I never know."

Samuel nodded and then walked out of the conference room. "I don't like this. Based upon the audio recordings, the targets are Grace and Dani."

"Any chance you can get them to leave town and stay gone until this is over?" Stan asked already knowing the answer.

"Not likely. Grace has a mid-term concert in three days. There's no way she'd miss that."

"Well then, we keep around the clock eyes on her and the kid. Did you talk to Trent?"

"Yeah. Sara's not happy, but he explained everything to her and she's agreed to not say anything to Grace right now. Hopefully they can get us a picture or a name to go on."

"Yeah. That would certainly help. James' driver played along beautifully when they stopped him last night. According to the information he provided me, James is planning on meeting with one of Julian's daughters later this month."

"Julian Quintana has a daughter? How old is she?"

"Don't know. Julian wants to see her, but aside from his lawyer, he's not allowed to receive any other visitors at this point in time. Sewell is filing a motion today to remove that restriction."

Samuel growled and then shook his head, "We can't let that happen. What's he using as evidence that he is no longer a threat?"

Stan laughed, "According to the driver, Julian has been a model citizen, and has gained the sympathy of some of the guards since Hector's death. Three of them had written letters of recommendation."

"They're dirty. They have to be on the take! No self-respecting peace officer would ever think Julian Quintana had changed that much."

"That's what I was thinking as well. I have a team digging through their personal files, but I doubt we'll find anything before the court hearing in," Stan looked at his watch and grimaced, "two hours."

Samuel shook his head and pinched the bridge of his nose. "Okay. I'm going to go talk to Michael. We need to bring him in on what's going on and as soon as Grace's concert is over, she's headed to Montana. Hopefully by the time the wedding is over, things will have calmed down around here."

"What about Jane?" Stan asked.

"Yeah, what about Jane? There's no way she's going to leave early. She's got too much going on at the test kitchen."

"Well, I don't know that it'll be safe for her to stay at Grace's house. Once Grace leaves town, we won't have leverage to keep surveillance on the place. She'd be a sitting duck."

"They don't know who she is though. That could work in our favor. I'll talk to her tonight. Maybe she could stay with Tori for a week or so?"

"That would work. She'd also be able to keep an eye on the house and let us know if anyone comes calling."

Samuel nodded and began making plans. He just needed to keep everyone safe until the trial. After that, it was lights out for both Trevor and Julian.

Chapter 20

Jackson showed up just as Grace and the girls were leaving for school. "Hey, what are you doing out so early?"

"I forgot to give you this envelope the other day when I dropped the dress off." Jackson walked across the driveway and handed her the envelope with a smile.

"Thanks. New ride?" Grace asked, eyeing the black SUV.

Jackson looked back at the SUV with a rueful grin, "Yeah, somehow I couldn't see the Mustang faring well in the mountains of Montana."

Grace laughed and shook her head, "Probably not. I couldn't believe how much snow they had up there at Christmas time."

"They got another foot just in the little bit of time I was up there," Jackson nodded his head. "I guess I'm probably gonna have to re-learn how to ski."

"Skiing? No thanks. I'll stick to the beach and sunscreen." She laughed and then hollered for the girls who were playing with Shelby in the front yard. "Emily. Dani. Time for school or you're going to be late."

"Hey, don't let me hold you up. I just found that last night and figured you were probably wondering what happened to it. That, and the fact that the movers are coming at the end of the week and I was afraid I would lose it in the mayhem that is sure to ensue."

"Hey, Mr. Jackson, watch this!" hollered Emily as she ran across the yard and attempted to do a front cartwheel. Unfortunately, her right arm buckled as she put it down and she cried out, landing in a heap in the grass.

Grace took off across the yard with Jackson right behind her, "Emily! Sweetie, don't move."

Jackson bent down next to the little girl, trying to keep her from moving too much until he could assess the situation. Emily pushed her legs out and then screamed in pain as she attempted to push herself up to a sitting position. She cradled her arm against her chest and her little body trembled in pain.

Jackson gave Grace a look and then nodded towards the house, "Can you go get Tori?" he whispered quietly. Grace nodded her head and took off running for the backyard. Her heart was racing and she couldn't believe this was happening.

Jackson could see Dani still standing in the middle of the yard with a look on her face that meant he was about to have two crying females to deal with. *Grace, come back quickly!* Seeing a little golden furball stick its head out from behind the gate, he pointed and sent Dani to stop the puppies from escaping. "Dani, sweetheart, can you go shut the gate and put that little guy in the backyard."

Dani followed his pointing hand and then nodded. That problem solved, Jackson turned back to the still crying Emily, although she was now shaking uncontrollably and he could see shock starting to set in.

"Emily, sweetie, does your arm hurt?" he asked softly, observing the angle of her arm and knowing that is was most definitely broken.

"Really bad," she said with a shaky voice.

"Emily!" Tori cried, coming out the front door and hurrying to where Emily sat in the grass.

Jackson looked up and shook his head, mouthing "Easy" to help calm her down. Tori's nurse training kicked in and he watched as she drew herself up and put a small smile on her face. "Hey, Grace tells me you were trying to be a gymnast."

"Mommy, it hurts!" Emily cried, reaching up with her good arm for her mother.

Tori knelt down in the grass and wrapped a tender arm around Emily's head. "I know, sweetie. Can you let Dr. Jackson look at your arm for a minute and then we'll go see the doctor and get you all fixed up."

"No!" Emily screamed. "No hospitals! You promised!"

Jackson looked up at Tori with a question on his face. She hurried to calm Emily down, "Sweetie, we need to go see the doctor so they can take a picture of your arm and fix it. Mommy will stay with you, okay?"

Emily let out a shuddering breath and then slowly nodded her head, the movement causing another rush of pain to push through her small body.

Tori looked up at Jackson with tears in her eyes, "I can't carry her."

"Shush, I'll do it. Grace, can you drive us to the hospital?" he asked calmly, dreading the moment when he would need to lift the little girl. Somehow, she had stolen a piece of his heart and the last thing in the world he wanted to do was cause her more pain.

Grace nodded and hurried to open the back door to her vehicle, "Dani, we need to go." She looked around and then at Jackson.

"I sent her to shut the gate and put the puppies back in."

Grace hurried over and retrieved Dani, thankful that the shock of her friend's injury was keeping her quiet. "We have to take Emily to the doctors. Can you get in your car seat, please?"

"Yes, mommy," Dani said, stopping to tell Emily, "The doctors will make you all better. Can we call Michael, mommy? Maybe he can stay with her so she won't be so scared like he did with me?"

"We'll see. Get in your car seat." Grace watched for a moment to make sure she could handle the task and then turned to Tori, "Let me help you up."

Once Tori was steady on her feet, Jackson made Emily look at him, "Sweetie, I'm gonna carry you to the car. I'm not going to lie to you, it's going to hurt when I pick you up, but I need you to be real brave for me. Can you do that?"

When Emily nodded, Jackson stood up and then bent over so he could lift her straight up, "Okay, here we go." Emily whimpered, but thankfully, she didn't cry out as he lifted her into his arms.

"Good girl. Just rest your head on my shoulder and close your eyes." He looked up to see Tori openly crying and told her, "She's going to be just fine. Let's get her to the hospital."

• • ❦ • •

"TORI, THE BREAK IS worse than I originally thought," the orthopedist told her. "The only way to ensure it will heal properly is to pin it."

"Surgery?" Grace asked, frowning when Tori nodded.

"I've already reserved the next surgery suite available. It shouldn't be long now. I'll send the nurse down with the paperwork."

Tori nodded her head, wondering why this was happening. At least they had sedated Emily and she appeared to be sleeping peacefully at the moment.

She was still lost in thought when the nurse arrived with the pre-op paperwork. Everything was fine until she came to the form suggesting someone with the same blood type make a donation, just in case something went wrong.

With this type of surgery, the possibilities of the patient needing a blood transfusion were extremely small, but it was standard procedure for every operation. Pulling the page out of order, she moved it to the back of the pile. Tori wasn't aware Jackson was looking over her shoulder until he asked, "You don't believe in giving blood. I would have thought someone with your training would have been all for that positive action."

"I can't give blood to Emily," Tori answered, continuing to focus on the paperwork. "I mean Emily can't use my blood. We're not the same blood type." Finding the donor paperwork, she thrust it at him and said, "Why don't you donate?"

"What makes you think Emily and I have the same blood type?" Jackson asked, starting to think maybe he was missing something big.

Tori looked at him and then set the pen down, "Jackson, I know why you didn't have closure with Michelle. It's okay. I'm not judging you, but if you really want to help, donate some blood. I doubt Emily will need it, but then again, nothing seems to be going right today."

Jackson was even more confused when Tori brought Michelle into the equation. "What does your sister have to do with my donating blood to your daughter?"

Tori looked at him and then it dawned on her that Jackson didn't know. She swallowed, wishing to be anywhere but here. "You didn't know, did you?"

"Know what?" Jackson sat down next to her, thankful that Grace had taken Dani to school and hadn't returned yet. "What is it that I didn't know?"

Tori closed her eyes and then whispered, "I'm not Emily's biological mom. I thought you knew and...," she opened her eyes and then looked away. "Jackson, Michelle was pregnant when we left Oregon."

She saw the shock on his face and then realized what he'd thought, "You thought I was the one with the baby?" When he nodded, she laughed, "That's a good one. The girl who's never been on a date gets accused of being promiscuous." She had tears running down her cheeks she was laughing so hard.

"Tori, I think there's been a big misunderstanding here. There is absolutely no way Emily is mine." When she looked at him and stopped laughing, he said it again, "None. Zero possibility."

"Then...," Tori trailed off, seeing the nurse returning for the paperwork. She handed it back to her, grateful when she left them alone once again. "If you weren't... I mean..."

"Look, I found out several months after graduation that Michelle had been dating a couple of guys from the next town over. Evidently, I wasn't exciting enough for her. The father has to have been one of them."

Tori was stunned. Jackson was angry that either of them had been put in this situation, and then her words came back to him. *The girl who's never been on a date...*

"How old were you when Emily was born?"

"Sixteen, why?" Tori asked, still trying to process this new information about her sister. She'd known her sister was out doing things she shouldn't do, but this...

"So, I want to make sure I haven't misunderstood anything else. Emily was born before the car accident?"

Tori shook her head, "No. Since Michelle was already thirty-five weeks along, they managed to keep her alive long enough to perform an emergency C-section. She died half an hour after delivery."

Jackson's admiration for the woman sitting next to him grew. "You were just a kid."

"I grew up fast. I didn't have a choice and I couldn't let them take her away."

"Tori," the orthopedist said, gaining her attention, "we're ready for her. I've already sedated her, so things should go pretty quickly. I'll come get you when she's out of surgery."

"Thanks, doctor." Tori watched him walk away and then turned to Jackson, "So you thought my mom had made us leave town because I had gotten pregnant?"

"Yeah, sorry."

"That's okay. Part of me wishes that had been true. After the chemo and radiation, my chances of ever getting pregnant are about ten percent."

"You still have Emily," Jackson reminded her.

"Yeah, that's something. I mean, don't get me wrong, I love that little girl as if she were my own. But what girl doesn't dream of having her own kids one day?"

"It could still happen. Ten percent isn't a zero percent."

Tori nodded her head, seeing Grace returning with Jane and Samuel in tow. *Amazing how nice it is to have friends!*

Chapter 21

Samuel chatted with Jackson while the women got up to speed on Emily's condition. He smiled when he heard Grace taking charge of things, "I've already called the women at the church, and they are going to bring meals for the next several weeks. With us all leaving in a few weeks for the wedding, I want to make sure you have plenty of help around. This will give you a chance to meet some new people."

Tori was so overwhelmed, she just sat there. Grace was taking over her life, and for now, that was okay with her. Emily came out of surgery forty-five minutes later and Jackson went back with Tori to sit with her in recovery.

Grace, Jane and Samuel promised to come up later and left to head their separate ways. Grace had a Children's Choir rehearsal and needed to be on time as it was the last one before their mid-term concert.

Samuel offered to drop Jane off at the test kitchen, needing a few minutes to explain what was happening with Julian and Trevor.

"So, you all think the lawyer is helping Julian set up a hit on Sara? But he's going to use Grace and Dani to find her?"

"That's a good summation of what we think is going on."

"So, if you followed him and know who the hit man is, why not just arrest them and be done with it?"

"If only it was that simple. We don't know what she looks like. No one does." Samuel's phone rang and he answered it, while he pulled over to the side of the road.

"Tell me some good news."

"Got it. We have a visual identification on the woman Sewell was calling the Raven. You're not going to believe who it is."

"Who?"

"Julian Quintana's daughter. She showed up on several South American watch lists."

"You're kidding me! Julian Quintana's daughter is the Raven?"

"Yep. We're going to take her down. She's either getting sloppy, or she thinks she's invincible. She left a trail a mile wide when she left the hospital. And get this, she was in the courtroom earlier today when Sewell made his plea for her father to start receiving visitors again."

"Where is she now?" Samuel asked, knowing that if they played their cards right, they could take her down before the sun set on this day.

"I have two cars following her. Shall we pick her up?" Stan asked.

"Do we have enough evidence to tie her to other crimes?"

"Not yet. But the driver left a message for me stating that Sewell expects the Sara situation to be resolved within forty-eight hours. If she's gonna grab Grace, it's gonna be soon."

"Have the team keep up the surveillance. We need to catch her in the act so that there's no chance of her making bail or getting off on a light sentence."

"That's what I was hoping you would say."

"Good. I'm going to stick with Jane, make sure both Grace and Dani have shadows today."

"Already done. See ya later."

Jane had listened calmly and then asked, "That's good news, right?"

"Yeah. I need you to keep Grace in the dark for a while longer. I don't want her acting different, or changing up her routine in any way. We need this woman to go after her or Dani..."

"But what if something goes wrong?"

"It won't. There's too much at stake, and they are so well covered, Dani can't hiccup without one of our team knowing about it."

Jane smiled at him, "I think the Raven should be very scared. It sounds as if her little reign of terror is about to come to an unpleasant end."

"That would be a blessing in many ways." *So many people have been hurt by her actions. It's time to end this!*

· · ✿ · ·

EMILY DID SO WELL IN recovery that she was able to go home with Tori about 5 o'clock that evening. Grace drove them all home since Jackson's SUV was still parked outside Grace's house.

Samuel and Jane were already at the house with Dani, when everyone arrived. Jackson carried Emily into the house, while Tori went ahead of him and turned down her bed. Jackson had offered to spend the night on the couch, and Tori had accepted without arguing.

Jane had left a casserole in the oven, and after making sure they didn't need anything else, Grace had headed home via the side gate.

She was halfway across the yard, when a female voice called to her from the street. Thinking that someone was lost and needed directions, she changed directions, but before she could take two steps, four dark sedans surrounded the vehicle and Stan was yelling at her to get down.

Grace didn't realize he was yelling at her, until she felt Samuel run up behind her and pull her to the ground. "Samuel? What's going on?"

"I'll explain everything later. For now, please just stay on the ground until we're sure she didn't bring help."

"Quintanas?" she asked, alarm keeping her down when Samuel nodded. Grace stayed on the ground, hoping Dani didn't try to come outside and see what all the flashing lights were about. Her bedroom was towards the back of the house, so hopefully she was still in princess mode and oblivious to everything else.

Jackson's voice came from behind the fence a moment later, "Samuel. You got everything under control?"

"Sure do. Just keep everyone inside for me."

"Done. I'm going to wait here. Whenever you feel it's safe enough, send Grace back towards me and I'll get her home."

"Dani's watching a movie in the house with Jane," Samuel informed him without taking his eyes off the motion on the street.

Moments later, Stan held up his hand and started across the grass, "She's working alone. We've got her dead to rights. She had both Grace and Dani's pictures, taped to her dashboard, and is singing like a lark. I'm thinking she doesn't know that we've figured out who she is, but she will. I'm saving that little piece of information for the right moment."

Samuel pulled Grace to a standing position, "It's all over now. With her confession and the other information we've gathered this last week, it should be enough to ensure Julian and Trevor get a 'Do Not Get Out Of Jail' card anytime in the near future."

"What will happen to her?" Grace asked, watching as two female agents cuffed the woman and placed her in the waiting vehicle.

"She's wanted in over a dozen countries. We'll get first stab at her, but I doubt we'll be able to hold her. She'll be extradited most likely over to the UK and they can deal with her."

Jackson, seeing that everything was under control, headed back indoors to find Tori standing near the living room window, watching the action.

"You should be lying down," he told her as he ushered her back to the couch.

"I saw the lights and was afraid they'd wake up Emily, but she's sleeping soundly."

"The pain meds they gave her should keep her sleeping off and on for the next few days. That will give you plenty of time to rest yourself."

Tori looked at him as he sat on the arm of the chair nearest the couch. "Thank you for everything you did today."

Jackson was quiet for a moment and then said, "Tori, I know this is going to sound weird, but I wish Emily was my daughter."

Tori looked at him in wonder, "Why?"

"Because then I'd have a valid reason to force my way into your lives. When your sister disappeared, a part of me left as well. I've had a few girlfriends over the years, but they were more like buddies, than romantic interests.

"I just couldn't convince myself to take a chance on love again. And before you say anything, I realize we were only seventeen, but I don't think it matters."

"What exactly are you trying to say?" Tori asked.

"I guess I want to be part of your lives. I know it probably sounds crazy..."

Tori shook her head, "Not really. I'd like to be friends."

Jackson looked at her and wanted so much more, but if a friend was all she could offer him right now, he'd make it be enough. He nodded and then told her, "I have a proposition for you and I need to know what you think about it before I make a phone call. Have you ever considered leaving California?"

Tori smiled, "So many times. Every time there's another shooting on the freeway, or I see a news story about a violent crime, I think about taking Emily and heading back to Oregon. But there's nothing there for me. We don't have any other family, and I doubt I could find work in a small town."

"But if the opportunity arose where you could raise Emily in a small town, you'd take it?"

"In a heartbeat. Why are you asking me these questions?"

"Well, I've been doing some thinking. You don't have a job holding you here, and the new clinic I'm going to be overseeing is going to need nurses. Nurses with experience in oncology."

Tori watched him and them asked, "Are they accepting applications? I've never been to Montana, but I'd be willing to look at it."

"Tori, you haven't been paying attention. I will be hiring the nurses and I just need to know if you would be interested. They haven't even broken ground on the building yet, but they are planning to be up and running by fall. I was wondering if you'd be interested in bringing Emily up and meeting some people and seeing the town."

Tori nodded, "Maybe. I don't know about flying, and with Emily's arm in a cast..."

"I'm already way ahead of you. Michael is flying Grace and Dani up for the wedding in his parent's private plane. There's plenty of room if you and Emily want to tag along and see the town. Talk to Sara and Bill Mercer and see if it's something you might want to explore further."

"But that's in just a few weeks," Tori exclaimed.

"I know. I have to be there by second of March, but you could come up the week after that and check everything out."

"Do you think Michael would mind a few extra passengers?" she asked, the thought of leaving California behind sounding more and more appealing.

"No, I don't. It would mean you couldn't have your surgery right away..."

Tori shook her head, "I'm not sure I can handle another one right away anyhow. I go to see Dr. Chevas next week and she's going to give me a few other options." Tori felt herself blushing and ducked her head.

"Tori, whatever you choose to do, I want to be there to offer support. I can help with Emily or whatever. Laundry. Dishes." Jackson smiled at her and she couldn't help but smile back.

"But you will be miles away in Montana by then," she reminded him.

"I can come back for a week or two."

Tori was silent for a moment and then nodded her head, "I'll come look at things if Michael has room for us."

Jackson, unable to stop himself, kissed her on the forehead, "I'll talk to him tomorrow. Now, dinner smells good. Ready to eat?"

Tori wasn't sure how she felt about Jackson's brief kiss. A funny feeling started in her stomach, and she passed it off as just being hungry. She nodded and got up from the couch, "I'm just going to go check on Emily. I'll be right back."

"I'll fix us a couple of plates."

Tori crept into her daughter's room and then knelt beside the bed. *Father, I know I haven't talked to you in the longest time, but if you can still hear me – I need your help. Please let Emily's arm heal right and take away her pain. And please help me decide which direction to go with my life.*

Tori spent a few minutes watching Emily sleep, before kissing her on the head and then lowering the light. She didn't know where her life was headed, but Jackson wanted to be a part of their lives and she didn't have the luxury of turning friends away. Maybe Montana would have a place for them as well.

Chapter 22

"Grace, you have a visitor?" Katelin told her as she hurried through their combined offices. The concert was slated to start in less than an hour, and the kids were already gathering downstairs.

Grace looked up and scowled, "Katelin, I don't have time for this tonight. Is it Michael? I'll text him and…"

"It's not Michael. Take five minutes and go downstairs. I promise you won't regret it." Katelin winked at her and then disappeared into their changing area.

Grace sighed and took one last glance in the mirror. Tonight's performance was being dedicated to Michael's parents on behalf of a grateful choir and their directors.

Grace hurried down the hallway and then stopped. Standing in the middle of the small foyer was none other than Sara and Trent. "Sara?" Grace queried, squealing as she'd done when she was eight.

She hurried down the hallway and threw herself into her sister's arms. "What are you doing here?"

Sara hugged her close and then pushed her away. "You look amazing!"

Grace threw her arms around Trent and hugged him just as tightly as she had her sister. "How did you?"

"Guilty," came the voice she loved. Turning around, she saw Michael leaning against the wall behind her with a smug look upon his face. "You didn't even miss me today, did you?"

Grace leapt into his arms when he held them open, "Thank you."

Michael kissed her and then set her back on her feet. "I figured after the excitement you've had, you deserved a little surprise. I flew up there this morning and met them and we just arrived back an hour ago."

"Oh, I can't believe you're here. How long are you staying?" Turning back to Michael, she asked, "How long can they stay?"

Everyone started laughing and then Trent answered, "We can stick around through tomorrow, but then we need to head home. Sara has the new director of the foundation..."

"Jackson, yes I know. Oh, we have got some catching up to do, sis. And you have to meet Tori and her daughter, Emily." Suddenly it dawned on her that she had no idea where her daughter was, if she wasn't with Michael. "Where is..."

"Dani's with my mom and dad. Brad and Teresa took her to their house after school and they have been playing grandma and grandpa all day. I'm not sure you're going to get her back after this. They're spoiling her something terrible."

Grace looked shocked and then started giggling, "How many tea parties have they had this afternoon?"

"Well, from what Brad was telling me, it wasn't the tea parties that got my dad. It was the makeup session..."

"She didn't! Oh, that little scamp is..."

"...a princess," Michael finished for her.

Grace smiled at everyone and then looked back down the hallway, "Guys, I really have to go get ready for the show. I'll see you all afterwards." She gave Sara and Trent another hug and then blew Michael a kiss. She was so happy, she found herself skipping down the hallway. This was going to be the best concert ever.

. . ⚜ . .

THE CONCERT WAS INDEED the best one the Southern California Children's Choir had ever put on and by the time Grace and her staff of helpers finished speaking to the grateful parents, her feet hurt, but her heart was full.

She'd had her very own cheering section in the audience consisting of current family and soon-to-be family. Jackson had brought Tori and Emily, the little girl making an amazing comeback from her broken arm and surgery.

Tori had been brave enough to wear her normally tight fitting clothing, so she'd opted for a pair of pants and a lightweight baggy sweater. She'd worn the short blonde wig, and been chauffeured to her seat in a borrowed wheelchair. Emily had shown everyone her cast, and Brad had produced a black marker, giving everyone a chance to write a special message to the little girl.

"Grace, I'm outta here. See you next week," Katelin hollered as she pushed her way out of the auditorium. With her departure, that left her and Michael and the cleaning crew.

"Are you ready to go?" Michael asked as she headed up the aisle towards him.

"Yes." Grace turned back and looked at the stage, "It was a good concert."

Michael wrapped his arms around her waist and rested his head on the top of hers, "It was fabulous. I don't think there was a dry eye in the place after the closing number."

"I love working with these kids. I had a thought during the concert. What if I found a way to incorporate music into your clinic? Music has such soothing properties. I would have to do some research into it, but..."

"That sounds perfect. I'll talk to Jackson and see what contacts he has. He specializes in alternative medicine and I'm sure he's run into the use of sensory stimulation as a form of therapy. For now, you look exhausted. Let me drive you home. Trent and Sara took Dani home hours ago."

Together, they turned and made their way out of the building. As they pulled away from the building, Grace sighed and let her eyes close. She was so blessed. Opening her eyes, she turned her head and looked at Michael and smiled. Sensing her stare, he reached for her hand and kissed her knuckles, "We're going to have a fabulous life together."

Grace nodded and smiled. *That about said it all! A fabulous life together!*

Chapter 23

"Mommy, does I has to go to school today?" a very sleepy little girl asked as she walked into the kitchen.

Grace held her arms out, smiling as Dani crawled up onto her lap and laid her head on her shoulder. Kissing her head, she wrapped her into a hug and said, "No. It's Saturday, so no school today. I thought maybe we would spend the day with Aunt Sara and Uncle Trent."

"Yay!" Dani scrambled down off her mother's lap and headed back down the hallway, "Aunt Sara! Wakes up! I gets to spend the whole day with you!"

Grace thought about calling her back and then shrugged. If they weren't already awake, they would be now! Five minutes later, Trent stumbled into the kitchen looking for coffee. When Grace handed him a fresh cup, he drank most of it before he looked at her and said, "I needed that. In fact, I might need another cup before I head back down the hallway. We were invited...no, invited isn't quite the right word..."

"Commanded. That's the word you're looking for," Grace offered, hiding her smile.

Trent thought for a moment and then nodded, "Yes! I do believe that is it! We were commanded to attend a tea party in Princess Daniella's room. What exactly did your daughter mean when she said I would look good in green?"

Grace burst out laughing, "Oh Trent. You are about to be welcomed to the family in royal style. I have to go get my camera for this." Grace was still laughing as she made her way back to the bedroom.

She saw Trent enter Dani's bedroom and decided to give him a few minutes to get properly attired for the party.

"Aunt Sara, come on!" Dani hollered from the bedroom, and Grace watched as a very sleepy Sara came out of the bedroom.

"Good morning, Sunshine!" Grace told her. "I do believe your presence is required by the princess of the house."

Sara smiled and then leaned against the wall, "What's the penalty for failure to appear?"

"Oh, somebody didn't get enough sleep. Come with me and we'll find you some coffee."

Sara shook her head, "Sorry, I'm off coffee for a while." She gave Grace a secretive look, waiting to see how long it would take for her comment to register. It didn't take long.

"You're pregnant?" Grace whispered. When Sara nodded her head, she grabbed her in a big hug. "Sara, that's wonderful. When's the baby due?"

"Around Thanksgiving. Will you come for the delivery?"

"You know I will. I'll even plan the fall concert schedule around it. Oh, I'm so happy for you."

"Trent's ecstatic. Speaking of which, I should probably go save him from Dani's evil clutches. I believe earrings and tiaras were mentioned."

"That they were. Here, take a picture to remember this moment by." Grace handed her the camera and then backed away. "I need to go next door and check on Tori."

"Wait, I want to come with you. Jackson mentioned that she might be interested in coming on board as the nurse supervisor and I didn't have a chance to talk to her last night. Let me snap a picture and then I'll be right back."

Grace headed for the kitchen, smiling when she heard a low, "Sara! Don't you dare! Sara, erase that picture now!" Seconds later, Sara rushed into the kitchen.

"Hide this and let's go." Grace stuffed the camera in the bread box and she and Sara stepped out of the house just before Trent could stop them. They were still chuckling when they entered Tori's back yard.

Jackson and Emily were sitting on the patio. Emily was scratching Shelby's head with her good arm, and Jackson was playing with the puppies.

"You didn't tell me they had puppies. Oh, I want one. Think Michael would mind me taking one back on the plane?"

"What about Trent? Won't he mind?" Grace asked,

"No! We talked about getting a puppy after the baby was born, but this would be even better. I could have the puppy housebroken before the baby came. I want a girl."

Emily had listened in and immediately pointed out a little girl pup who was sitting quietly, watching her brothers bite on each other's tails. "She's really sweet. Dani and I named her Beauty."

Sara picked up the puppy, giggling when she received a bath from the little puppy tongue. "Oh, she's mine. Are they ready to go to new homes yet?"

Jackson nodded, "Yeah, they have been for a week, but Tori and Emily have been having a hard time letting them go."

Sara felt something bite her toes and looked down to see a roly-poly little puppy, trying to get her big toe into its mouth. "Oh, goodness. What's this one's name?"

Emily looked at the biggest puppy of the litter and laughed, "Olly. Watch out, if he gets your toe into his mouth, it really hurts."

Sara could feel the little needles sinking into her toe and she fell in love. "Okay, two puppies would keep each other company, right?"

"Are you trying to convince me, or yourself?" Grace asked.

"Emily, how much are you asking for the puppies?"

"Nothing from you," Tori told her from the backdoor. "If your husband is okay with you taking two of them home, please do."

Sara shook her head, "No way! You can tell me what you want for them and I'll pay the going rate."

Tori got a militant look in her eye. "We'll talk."

"That's why I'm here actually. Is now a good time?" Sara asked, putting the puppy in her arms down and then picking up the little boy dog and loving on him for a few minutes.

"Sure. What did you want to talk about?" Tori asked, puzzled why someone she'd just met the evening before wanted to talk to her.

"Jackson and I spoke briefly and he mentioned you were looking for a new job. With your experience, I am here to convince you to move to Montana and supervise the nursing staff."

Tori was stunned. "But you just met me?"

Sara smiled at her. "And I am an excellent judge of character."

Tori stepped back, "Well then, I guess you'd better come in and tell me what I'll be missing if I don't accept your kind offer."

"Sara, I'm going to go rescue Trent. Emily, want to come to my house for a bit?" Grace asked, wanting to give the three adults plenty of time to work everything out. She would miss Tori and Emily, but in her heart of hearts, she knew that they needed to go to Montana. Just like Sara had needed to go to Montana. It was a magical place where people could heal and get a second chance at finding true happiness.

Chapter 24

Castle Peaks, Montana, March 15th...

The chapel was filled to overflowing as everyone in the community had come out to see Jane get married. She and Samuel had arrived in town six days prior and everything had led up to this one event. The wedding of Jane Trowler to Samuel Drackett.

Grace and Dani had flown in three days prior, along with Tori, Emily, and the remaining four puppies and their momma. Emily's arm was still in a cast, and would be for another three weeks, or until the x-rays showed the bones had healed enough the pins could be removed. It didn't seem to slow her down at all.

Tori had agreed, to seriously consider moving to Montana, and was planning on making her final decision before Michael flew them back to California. As far as her recovery went, she had a clean bill of health and had met with Dr. Chevas, but had decided against further surgery. Instead, she had been fitted for a special undergarment which would help compensate for the disfigurement left behind by the cancer.

Grace and Michael had taken two of the puppies, which were currently residing with his parents for the weekend. When they were old enough, they were going to train them to be therapy dogs and incorporate them into the new pediatric cancer clinic.

One of Grace's coworkers had taken the last puppy, as the four that had travelled to Montana had been spoken for as soon as Sara and Trent had arrived with their two additions.

A fresh blanket of snow had fallen the night before, and Trent smiled as he readied the horse drawn sleigh behind the church. Spring was just around the corner, but today it still looked like winter.

Samuel had managed to pull some strings and gained his superior's blessing to use the FBI safe-house just outside of town as a honeymoon getaway. Jane had no idea what he had planned and Trent smiled as he remembered how happy she had looked last night at the rehearsal dinner. For so many years Jane had been a part of his family, and her happiness meant the world to him.

Dani was playing the flower girl, and after much negotiation between her mother and Aunt Jane, she had consented to only wearing her princess attire for the rehearsal dinner; not the actual wedding. The little girl stole everyone's heart that she met, Trent's included.

Trent pushed through the back door of the chapel, stamping his feet to rid them of the snow before he tracked it down the long hallway. "Trent," Pastor Jameson called to him from a side room.

"Hi Pastor. Everything ready in here?" Trent asked as he stepped into the small office the Pastor used to get ready for the weekly sermons.

"Looks like it. I think the entire town has shown up."

"Good. I heard Grace working with the children's choir a little while ago. They sounded fantastic."

"She is so good with them. I can see why she is so successful out in California. It was nice of her to send the music out ahead of time."

"Sometimes I feel like the luckiest man in the world. I found a wonderful wife, who has a wonderful sister and niece."

Pastor Jameson nodded his head. "And did I hear correctly that you and Sara will be welcoming a new little one around Thanksgiving?"

Trent grinned and chuckled, "That you did. It might take us that long to get those two puppies trained. This week alone they chewed up two pair of shoes, and last night, they managed to get into the pantry and they broke open a bag of flour. I guess I forgot to shut the door all the way."

Pastor Jameson laughed, imaging the mess they must have created. "Well, at least it was only flour. It vacuums up. It could have been syrup."

Trent laughed with him, "They have now earned the right of staying in the laundry room when we are out for more than a few minutes. I never imagined they could get into so much mischief."

"Mischief? Who's getting into mischief?" Samuel asked, stepping into the room.

"The puppies. The sleigh's all ready to go out back. Jeb's going to bring the horses over just as soon as the ceremony's over. That wind is way too cold for them horses to stand out there."

"What is up with the wind? I was hoping things would have warmed up around here."

Trent laughed, "You've spent too many years in California. This is warm."

"I'm perfectly happy there, thanks." Samuel couldn't imagine living in these snowy conditions for months on end. He'd go stir crazy!

"Are the girls doing okay?" Trent asked.

"As far as I know. They spirited Jane away yesterday after the rehearsal dinner and I haven't even been able to talk to her. What if she's changed her mind?"

"You know better than that. She didn't wait all those years to get cold feet now. Speaking of which, I need to go change out of these wet boots. I'll see you up front in a few minutes."

· · ⚛ · ·

JACKSON SAT TOWARDS the back of the sanctuary with Emily on one side and Tori on the other. He glanced down at her and couldn't help but smile. Seeing a shadow stop next to their pew, he looked up to see a kindly older woman smiling at them, "You have a lovely family. I heard you were the new doctor for the clinic Bill's building. Welcome to Castle Peaks. I hope your wife and daughter will be happy here."

Before Jackson or Tori could correct her, she ambled down the aisle. Jackson looked at Tori, who was looking at the woman with a wistful look upon her face.

"So, have you given Sara's offer anymore thought?" he asked, having restrained himself from asking these last few days.

Sara nodded, "This is such a nice town. I could see us living here, but the lady that owns the B&B said there aren't any vacant houses or apartments in town."

"There's not, but I have a solution to that. But before I mention it, I want to know if you're going to take the job as nursing director."

Sara smiled at him, "I think so. Emily and I talked about it last night, and she thinks it might be fun to try living in a new place. Isn't that so?"

Emily nodded her head, "I want to learn to ski. Mr. Trent said he could teach me if we lived here."

"He probably could, but not until next winter. That arm needs plenty of time to heal before you go barreling down a mountainside." Jackson waited for her to agree, nudging her when she did.

"So, does that mean I can tell Sara you'll take the job?" Jackson asked.

Sara's head popped right between them, "I heard my name. Did she say 'Yes' yet?"

"She was just about to give me an answer to the first question, but you interrupted us."

Sara murmured, "Sorry", and then stared at Tori. "Well?"

"Fine. I would love to take the job."

Sara smiled, "Great! We'll talk details before you all head home." Turning to Jackson, she nodded at Tori, "Ask her the second question."

Jackson gave an exasperated sigh and told her, "When I'm ready. Don't you have a husband waiting for you somewhere and a bride to lead down the aisle?"

"My, my, you're cranky."

Tori watched the two interact and then swallowed when Jackson turned the full weight of his stare on her. Moistening her lips, she asked softly, "What's the second question?"

Jackson looked to see if the wedding was about to start and then looked at her again. "You've seen that big old house I'm living in. It was built with a family in mind. I know you said we could be friends, but I think we could be much more than that." Seeing she was about to speak, he laid a gentle finger over her lips, "Let me finish."

"I think you and Emily should move into the house with me. You can have the ground level, and I'll stay in one of the upstairs rooms. It will give us a chance to get to know each other and give Emily a place to live."

"Are you asking me to move in with you?" Tori asked.

"Yes, but not in the way you're thinking. I'm asking you to become my roommate while we discover if we could ever be more than that. We could share expenses, and the cooking and such. We could work things out so that you and Emily were comfortable with the arrangement."

"Won't the townspeople think poorly of us both if we were to live together without being married?" Tori asked, remembering all of the judgmental comments her mother had made during her formative years. She didn't want to be on the receiving end of those types of statements.

"Actually, Bill Mercer was the one who suggested it. As a trial basis, of course. He's already planning to build some smaller homes just outside of town, but not until the clinic is finished. That means those houses wouldn't be ready to move into until late fall."

"Where will the other employees live then?" Tori asked, already thinking ahead and from a logistical standpoint, something would need to be done to provide temporary housing for others who moved to Castle Peaks.

"Bill's going to have some temporary trailers brought up from Butte once the snow melts. It won't be the nicest accommodation, but it will do until the houses are completed."

"Mommy, I want to live in the house with the big tree fort in the backyard. Can we do that? For just a little while?"

Tori started to answer him, but the music changed, indicating the wedding was about to begin. "We'll have to talk about this some more."

Chapter 25

"Okay Dani, do it just like we practiced. Step. Together. Flowers. Step. Together. Flowers." Sara told the darling little girl in front of her.

Dani had begrudgingly agreed to forego the princess attire for this afternoon's event, and Sara hadn't been able to stand the sad look on her face. She'd sent Trent back to the house and had him locate the green tiara amongst the costume jewelry and bring it to the church. She'd already discussed it with Jane, who'd readily agreed, that as long as Samuel didn't have to wear it, Dani was welcome to.

Dani smiled at her and whispered loudly, "I's remember. And I can't throw the flowers at the peoples, but I need to drop them on the ground."

Sara bit her lip, "That's perfect, sweetie. Okay, go ahead."

Everyone turned and watched as Daniella began her trek down the aisle. She did an excellent job of walking slowly, smiling at the guests, and dropping the flowers onto the floor. Until she reached the halfway point that is. Several of the older ladies had been whispering loudly about how adorable she was, and Daniella had decided to play it to the hilt. Instead of walking sedately now, she was twirling and curtsying, every other step, much to the amusement of everyone in attendance. Even Grace was trying not to laugh, but losing the battle.

When she reached the front, she was supposed to have a seat on the front pew next to her mother and Michael. True to form, Daniella decided to hold court instead. Gaining the front of the aisle, she curtsied to Samuel, who played along, bowed, and winked at her.

She then turned to the waiting guests and regally inclined her head at both sides of the sanctuary, causing the entire congregation to erupt in laughter. Having no idea that she was the reason for the merriment, she then walked sedately over and sat down on the pew, folding her hands in her lap quietly.

Sara and Jane were both laughing so hard, they had tears running down their faces. "I'm glad we used the waterproof mascara, or your wedding pictures would have a couple of raccoons in them."

Jane managed to control her laughter and then smiled, "I wouldn't care. I've never seen one little girl control a crowd like that. She definitely needs to act on the stage."

"Either that or marry a prince with a country to run," Sara added, wondering when her niece was finally going to give up on the princess routine. *Hopefully no time soon! That was priceless!*

The children's choir took their places and began the song that signaled it was time for Sara to walk down the aisle. As Trent was Samuel's best man, Sara had a chance to reminisce about her own wedding. She watched Trent as she walked towards him, unconsciously placing a hand over the new life that was growing inside of her.

She didn't see the knowing looks that passed between the guests, or the smiles that were directed at her as she passed by them. She had eyes only for her husband. Gaining the front of the church, she too decided to deviate from the prescribed program and approached Trent with a small smile upon her face.

"I am so glad I married you," she whispered to him as he leaned down to greet her with a kiss.

"I love you, Sara." Trent's eyes were shining with love and as he gently touched her cheeks, couples throughout the congregation held onto each other's hands, letting each other know how they felt without words.

Sara kissed him one more time and then headed to take her place at the left of the altar. When she glanced back and saw Jane watching her in bemusement, she shrugged and giggled.

The children's choir finished their song and the organist began to play the traditional wedding march. The congregation stood and Jane began her walk down the aisle. Samuel moved to stand in the middle, so that she walked straight towards him.

He was so handsome, it took her breath away. She let her eyes move over his face, trying to record every nuance of this moment, to be pulled out and viewed at a later date and time.

Samuel watched Jane walk towards him with a smile meant only for him. Her dress was absolutely stunning. A soft peach color, it fell in soft waves around her body, with a hem that was shorter in the front, and then elongated in the back until it hit the floor and created a train behind her.

She'd declined wearing a veil, wanting nothing between her and Samuel when she arrived at the altar. Samuel was the fulfillment of her dreams. Her saving grace and the reason she had so much joy in her life.

Samuel took her hand when she reached him and then turned her to face Pastor Jameson. Trent's parents had been unable to return in time for the wedding, but had sent their fondest wishes for her happiness, and had promised to stop in California before returning home. Several men in the community had offered to give Jane away, but she'd declined them all saying, "No one is giving me away. I am freely giving myself to Samuel."

Pastor Jameson looked at the couple before him with a smile and then back out at the audience, "We are gathered together today, to witness the union of Samuel Drackett to Jane Trowler. Marriage is..."

Chapter 26

Jane listened to Pastor Jameson go through his "What Marriage Is" speech, but her mind was on the future. Samuel hadn't told her where they were going for their honeymoon, and he hadn't let her pack. Gracie had packed her suitcase for the honeymoon, per Samuel's instructions, and she had absolutely no idea where they were headed.

"Are you listening, or daydreaming?" he whispered softly to her.

Jane glanced up at him and smiled. "A little of both."

"Jane, do you take Samuel as your lawfully wedded husband? To have and to hold, from this day forward, in sickness and in health, until in death you shall part?"

Jane met Samuel's eyes and nodded, "I do."

"Samuel, do you take Jane to be your lawfully wedded wife? To love and protect, to cherish and support, not matter what may come, from here into eternity?"

Samuel watched Jane's eyes as she listened to the words, "I do." He had written his own vows, wanting to make sure she understood exactly what she meant to him. He saw the tears make her eyes shine and whispered to her, "I didn't mean to make you cry."

"That was beautiful."

Pastor Jameson could tell the couple needed just a moment so he paused to retrieve the rings from Trent and Sara. Once he held them in his hand, he continued the ceremony, pleased to see that Jane had pulled herself back together.

Pastor Jameson prayed over the rings and then watched as they placed the rings upon each other's finger, repeating the words, "With this ring, I thee wed."

"...you may now kiss the bride," was the last thing Jane heard before Samuel swept her into his arms and proceeded to kiss her senseless. When Pastor

Jameson coughed behind them, Samuel finally let her up, to the applause of the congregation.

Not to be outdone, Daniella immediately presented herself in front of Samuel and demanded to be lifted up, "My turn."

Samuel laughed, but picked her up and kissed her on the tip of her nose before handing her off to a blushing Grace.

Taking Jane's hand, he led her down the aisle and then pulled her around the corner for a moment of privacy. "Jane, I love you."

"I love you too. Thank you for making my dreams come true."

Samuel leaned down and kissed her once more. As they broke apart, Trent and Sara were there, urging them to get in place for the receiving line. It was decided that after they had greeted their guests, Samuel would slip Jane out the back door and they would head towards the cabin. Trent and Sara would play host and hostess during the reception in their stead.

Fifty minutes later, the last guest had wished them well and Samuel pushed Jane in Sara's direction, "Go with her."

"Go where?" Jane asked.

"Come on. Where doesn't matter. It's with whom that does." Sara led her back to the bride's room where Grace had her suitcase open and was pulling out jeans, a warm sweater, her mittens, scarf and gloves. Her winter coat lay draped over a chair, and her snow boots stood beneath it.

"I guess I'm not heading for a beach," she commented to the two women.

"No. Not the beach. Come on, we need to get you changed."

Ten minutes later, a much warmly dressed Jane was directed to find Samuel by the back door of the chapel. "Hey," she called to him, seeing that he too had changed into winter clothing.

"Hey, my beautiful wife. Are you ready to get out of here?"

"I think so. Where are we going?"

"Wait and see. Now, close your eyes," he urged.

Jane complied and put her trust in his direction. She felt when they stepped outside, the cold wind biting her cheeks and making her shiver. "Okay, you can open them now."

Jane opened her eyes and then gasped. A horse-drawn sleigh stood waiting on them, complete with a driver and warm blankets to snuggle under. "Samuel, it's gorgeous."

"I'm glad you like it. Let's go. Those blankets looked nice and warm." Samuel handed her up into the sleigh and then arranged several of the warm blankets around them both. When she naturally snuggled up against his chest, he didn't think his world could get much better.

. . ∞ . .

TRENT AND SARA GREETED everyone at the reception, letting them know that the bride and groom wished them all well, and hoped to see them the next time they were in town. There were a few disappointed people, but for the most part, they completely understood the couple's desire to be alone.

Word started to spread through the reception hall that Sara was expecting, and Trent found himself making an announcement to that effect in place of the traditional groomsman's toast. The gathered townsfolk were elated and it provided yet another reason to celebrate.

Jackson steered Tori to an empty table, having assigned Emily to a table full of other kids her age who lived in town. After grabbing them two plates of cake and some punch, he leveled her with a stare and boldly asked, "Would you consider sharing my house and seeing if we have anything other than friendship?"

Tori had thought of nothing else since he'd asked. During the beginning part of the ceremony, when Sara had walked down and kissed Trent so sweetly, she'd felt tears come to her eyes.

Somehow, Jackson had picked up on the emotion, and had taken her hand in his, keeping it clasped between them the remainder of the ceremony. Just having his holding her hand had given her a peace that had been missing for years. She hadn't felt alone or inadequate. She'd felt a part of something and that wasn't a feeling she wanted to let go of.

Tori looked at him, "What if we find we just don't get along with each other?"

"I've already thought of that. Bill offered me a room in his house if things become too weird or too uncomfortable. I think the secret to making this work is communication. We need to talk to each other."

"And what do we tell Emily?"

"The truth. That we're going to be roommates and share that big old house for a while. If friendship turns into something else; then we'll tell her that when the time comes."

"You have this all figured out, haven't you?" Tori asked.

"I've thought of nothing else since you said 'Goodbye' to me two weeks ago."

Tori thought back to that morning and blushed. Jackson had stopped by the house to tell them both "Goodbye" before he headed out. In a rash moment, Tori had flung herself into his arms and hugged him tight. The hug had led to a kiss of monumental proportions, leaving them both breathless and speechless.

Since that kiss, neither of them had mentioned it. They had spent hours on the phone talking, but the kiss had remained a non-subject. It appeared that pretending it hadn't occurred, was not the same thing as actually making it disappear.

"So what are you saying?" Tori asked.

"I'm saying that I want more than friendship with you, but I'll settle for whatever you feel you can give me right now. If friendship is all you can handle, then that's where we'll start. But I warn you, I am going to do everything in my power to change your mind."

Tori wanted him to change her mind. "So how... I mean..."

"How would we go about this?" When she nodded, he pulled out the second part of his plan, "Tori, I want to take you on a date."

"A date? But I thought..."

"A date. Just because we're going to be sharing a house, doesn't mean we can't have a normal relationship. When you get settled in, I want to take you out on a date. We'll get Trent and Sara to watch Emily, and go to dinner or see a movie. Just the two of us."

Tori swallowed, "You know I've never done any of this?"

"All the more reason for me to make sure you don't miss a thing. So what do you say, will you go out with me?"

"Yes. Jackson, I would love to go out with you."

Jackson smiled at her and then kissed her briefly on the mouth, "Yep, I wasn't imagining the fireworks the last time. They're still there. When did you say you and Emily were moving up here?"

• • ⌘ • •

JEB STEERED THE SLEIGH to the safe house, stopping as close to the porch as possible and then helping Samuel and Jane alight. "I'll be back in three days. You two lovebirds enjoy."

Samuel stood with Jane wrapped in his arms until the sleigh was out of sight. Turning, he looked up at the house, thankful that someone had already lit a fire in the hearth and then banked it. "Cold?"

Jane shivered, "Yes. You know, I never seemed to feel the cold when I lived here all the time. I must be getting used to the warm weather."

"Well, let's get inside then." Samuel placed his hand on her lower back and guided her up the stairs. When they reached the front door he opened it, but when she would have walked through, he stopped her.

Scooping her up in his arms, he grinned at her and said, "I intend to start as I mean to continue. Welcome to your temporary home Mrs. Drackett."

He stepped through the door and then kicked it shut behind him. He could tell Sara and Grace had been hard at work. There were little feminine touches everywhere he looked, and he was most certain that the FBI agents who'd last used the house hadn't left them there.

"Samuel, this is amazing. You did get permission for us to be here, right?"

Samuel looked at her and then nodded, "How do you know what this place is?"

Jane smiled at him, "Samuel, I've lived in Castle Peaks a long time. Something like this might have escaped the notice of normal people, but my nephew is the town sheriff. I know all sorts of things about this town."

Samuel laughed and set her down, "Well, I'll make you a deal. You keep my secrets, and I won't tell those three chefs what you put in your chocolate sauce."

Jane nodded her head, "Deal." She watched as he removed his coat and she did the same. "So, whatever are we going to do up here for three days?"

Samuel toed off his boots and then gave her a look that said he definitely had some ideas. Loving the way they could banter with one another, he teased her, "Trent said there are several board games in that cabinet and a deck of cards. Want to play a game?"

Jane finished removing her boots and approached him on silent feet, "Maybe later. Right now, I would like to get to know my husband better."

Samuel picked her up in his arms once again and headed down the hallway. "That sounds like an excellent idea."

Epilogue

Castle Peaks, Montana, Thanksgiving Day...

"Uncle Trent, how come baby Mari can't sit up by herself?" Dani asked, still totally enthralled with her newborn cousin.

"Well, sweetie, when you were this little, you couldn't sit up either. But don't you worry, Mari will grow up big and strong just like you and be able to do all sorts of things."

Daniella looked at the baby cradled in Trent's arm dubiously, but then Emily came through the front door and the baby was forgotten.

"Hey Dani. Come see what I brought," Emily told her. The two girls disappeared into the den as Jackson escorted Tori into the living area of the house.

Tori held her hands out, "Give her to me. You can hold her anytime you like."

Trent handed his daughter over and watched as Jackson and Tori loved on her. "So, did I hear that you two finally decided to stop sharing that house?"

Tori looked at Jackson and then smiled, "Yes. We're still going to live together, but as a family. Jackson asked me to marry him last night and I agreed. We're going to get married right after the first of the year."

"Did I hear someone mention a wedding in here?" Grace asked, wiping her hands on a towel as she greeted Tori and Jackson.

"Yep. I finally got her to agree to marry me."

"Well, it's about time. I was beginning to wonder about you two."

Jackson smiled, "No worries here. Now that the clinic is up and running, we should have plenty of time to pull a wedding together."

Sara smiled, "I'm getting pretty good at organizing them. I'm happy to help wherever I can."

"Thanks, Sara. How are you feeling?" Tori asked, amazed at how good Sara looked for having just had a baby a few days ago.

"I'm feeling really good. A little tired, but this little one doesn't have a very good schedule yet. She seems to have her days and her nights mixed up."

"That happens. When Emily was an infant, I would find myself keeping her up, even upsetting her to keep her awake, just so that I could get more than two hours of sleep in a row. Believe me, the sooner she figures out that she needs to sleep when it's dark outside, the better everyone will feel."

"I tried that a little yesterday, and I actually got to sleep for four hours before she woke me up. I figured I could always sleep during the day when she does, but then I'd be awake all night."

Jane came through the door just then, "Happy Thanksgiving everyone."

"Where's Samuel and Michael?" Jackson asked, just figuring out that they were noticeably absent.

"They went out to cut down a Christmas tree," Jane glanced at the clock above the mantle, "three hours ago. They should be back any time now." When she heard the back door slam shut, she smiled, "And there they are."

"Hey babe, we got an absolutely gorgeous tree. Trent, did you find that stand we were talking about?"

Trent nodded, "Yeah, Let me get it and we can bring the tree in before dinner."

"I'll come with you," Jackson said, leaving the room right after Trent.

The women all looked at each other and then burst into giggles, "Should we be worried that they think it will take four grown men to install a tree stand?"

"No. If they don't come back before dinner's ready, we'll send Emily and Daniella out to help them."

"Happy Thanksgiving," called Trent's parents from the front door. David and Deirdre Harding had missed their son and Jane's wedding as they were on a world cruise. They had arrived back home in late June. After stopping in California to meet Samuel and Sara's sister, they had come back to Montana and settled down.

More hugs ensued and then David realized he was the only man still in the room. "Where are they?"

That question caused more giggles and he watched in amusement as they attempted to tell him where the men had gone. Finally understanding them, he headed outside to lend his expert advice on how to install a tree stand on a Christmas tree.

"Let's get the rest of dinner on the table," Jane suggested.

The women made short work of carrying the multitude of dishes to the table. There were multiple vegetables, turkey and ham, three varieties of potatoes, and salads galore. It seemed everyone had contributed their favorite to the meal.

After everyone was seated around the table, Trent prayed and then they each took a turn publicly giving thanks for something in their lives.

"I'm thankful for a healthy baby girl," Sara said when it became her turn.

"I'm thankful to be cancer free," said Tori.

"I'm thankful for the opportunity to help so many people," said Jackson.

Each person took their turn, and then they started dishing up the food. At one point during the meal, Sara glanced up and looked around the table.

She had found her soul mate in Montana. Jane had found the answer to her dreams in California. Grace had met her perfect man in California. And then there was Jackson and Tori.

They had first met in California, but Montana had brought them truly together. Without a place to meet in Montana and an opportunity to get to know one another better, they wouldn't be planning a wedding. They truly were a couple that had met in two different places, but had attained the same goal. Someone who understands you to go through life with.

She looked around the table and watched her friends and family members interact. Jane and Samuel were expecting their first child. Jane was a natural caregiver and Sara knew she would make a wonderful mom.

Yes, life in Montana had been good not only to her, but to those around her. Sensing Trent watching her, she gave him a smile and then kissed their daughter. Life was full of surprises, but only the best ones seemed to be born in Montana. The place where dreams can become reality, and second chances are always given.

. . ❧ . .

DID YOU LOVE *New Beginnings*? Then you should read the complete set of all 6 books in *Second Chances Series* by Morris Fenris. You can grab Book 4, *Second Time Around*, here: https://books2read.com/u/mZrpqe

. . ❧ . .

Prologue

S *an Diego, California, mid-October...*

Bryan Jackson pushed the glass doors open and stepped out into the sunshine, wishing his soul didn't feel so dark and heavy. He was finally back in Southern California, after spending the last two years working undercover for the FBI trying to take down a drug trafficking ring. Well, it had started out that way at least; but after working his way into the inner circle of the South American cartel, he'd come to realize they were trafficking things much more valuable than drugs. They'd been trafficking humans! Defenseless women to be more precise. The idea of it still sent fire roaring through his veins.

After living more like an animal than a man, every day an affront to his sense of right and wrong, seeing and doing things he hoped he would be able to forget someday, the trafficking ring had finally been taken down and his part of the operation was over. *Thank God!*

All but the grandson of the cartel's leader—Emilio Arrelano—had been killed during the massive raid that had taken place a month earlier. Eduardo Arrelano was only nineteen, but had committed crimes far beyond his years, and in Bryan's opinion his soul was truly evil. Not that it would matter much in the next ninety-six years; the length of time he'd been sentenced to serve in federal prison for his part in the activities of the cartel.

Bryan had given his testimony in court earlier today at the sentencing hearing, sealing the young man's fate by suggesting that letting Eduardo free in this lifetime would be a blight on society and truly wrong. The judge had agreed. Bryan was happy the cartel was no longer in operation, but not naive enough to believe another wouldn't rise up to take its place soon enough. Maybe it already had.

His director had hinted that he might be the ideal candidate to try and take down the next group, but Bryan had simply shaken his head and walked out of the building. That had been two days ago, and he'd not heard anything more about going back into deep cover. As he headed for his office, he made up his mind on the way there. He needed a vacation. Now!

He walked into the San Diego FBI office and accepted the congratulations from his co-workers and support staff for a job well done. He nodded and returned their greetings with a tight smile. He didn't feel like celebrating, even knowing that he had accomplished his goal and taken apart the cartel. He'd seen too much and it was going to be hard to forget.

He wrapped his knuckles on Director Kennedy's door, then went inside when the man waved him forward.

"Good job today. One less criminal on the streets."

"Eduardo Arrelano was much more than a common criminal. If he were to ever get out, just his name and lineage alone would create a level of chaos that no one needs." Bryan lowered himself carefully into the leather chair situated in front of the massive desk. He schooled his features so that no hint of the pain he was feeling showed.

As far as everyone at the bureau was concerned, he'd been given a clean bill of health. No one knew that he'd developed a secondary infection in the wound two weeks after he'd been treated at the local hospital, and he wanted to keep it that way. He'd intentionally gone to an after-hours clinic and paid cash to have the wound irrigated and get some antibiotics. The last thing he needed was to have the FBI's special medical team looking over his shoulder again. It was annoying, and in his opinion, unnecessary.

"Well, I've heard they're going to be transferring him up tonight. He'll be assigned to Atwater and it's already been discussed that if he becomes a problem there, he'll be transferred to the ADX penitentiary in Florence, Colorado."

Bryan nodded, "Let's hope that doesn't happen. Unless things have changed, there aren't that many non-lifers at Florence, and Eduardo doesn't need anyone giving him ideas about escaping. At nineteen, he's a quick study and given just a little leeway, he could easily get enough backers inside to be a threat."

Director Kennedy looked at him and cocked his head to the side, "Have you read the psychologist's latest report on him?"

Bryan shook his head, "No, I read the initial assessment. I saw no reason to read the follow-up, I already know the kid's a psychopath who, to quote the shrink, *'shows no remorse nor does he seem to value human life, including his own.'* Why?" The actual trial had been over ten days earlier, but the sentencing hearing had been postponed due to other court business.

Kennedy shrugged and then shook his head, "No reason, I guess. Eduardo is claiming he's a changed man after meeting with one of the prison chaplains. He's found God." Kennedy's voice was full of derision and mockery.

Bryan raised a brow, "Really?" Bryan had been raised in a good Christian home and didn't discount the ability of God to completely change a person's life around, but Eduardo Arrelano? Yeah, that one he was definitely having some trouble with. He'd seen the young man at work, and a more vile and evil person had only existed while Eduardo's grandfather Emilio was still alive. Taking a breath, he commented, "Nothing was discussed at the sentencing hearing today about that, seems like his defense attorney would have tried to get him a lighter sentence..."

"Eduardo refused to let him. He said he deserved the same penalty that the rest of his family and friends received, and that if God let him live, then it was for a reason, and he was going to spend the rest of his life trying to help others see the light."

Bryan huffed out a harsh laugh.

"In Atwater? Good luck with that. He'll be lucky if someone doesn't kill him the first week he's in the general population." Murderers and those that had committed horrible crimes had a unique aversion to anyone who preyed on women or children. Especially young women that were more child than adult. It was a well-known fact, and the reason most child predators who received life sentences did so in a solitary state for the most part.

Kennedy nodded, "From what I hear, they're going to be keeping a close eye on him for the next several months. Who knows, maybe he truly has seen the light." Bryan never discounted the power of God, having seen more than a few miracles in his lifetime. But Eduardo Arrelano was pure evil and about as irredeemable a person as Bryan had ever met.

Pausing for a moment, Kennedy changed the subject, "But enough about criminals, I'm guessing you're not here to discuss going back undercover?"

Bryan rolled his shoulders, "I'm out." He knew his decision wasn't going to be a popular one, but his sanity was at risk here.

"Out?" Kennedy asked, focusing his gaze on the steeple he was making with his hands on his desk. "Explain, please?" Director Kennedy was a 6'6," broad-shouldered, black man whose mere physical appearance was intimidating. When he lowered his voice and demanded an explanation, even seasoned agents like Bryan felt the full force of the man's authority. But Bryan wasn't backing down. Not this time.

"I need some time off to...I don't know, find myself again. Having to pretend to be like those animals...I don't know, I feel like I've lost part of my humanity." He'd had to pretend to be a hardened, ruthless killer to get close enough to the Arrelano family to take the cartel down. He'd gone in as an enforcer, knowing he'd have little to no trouble ridding the Earth of evil men. He hadn't figured on the innocent women, some of them still more child than adult. While he'd managed to avoid committing any truly heinous acts during his two years undercover, he'd been forced to stand by and watch as others did the unthinkable. Time and again.

It was all part of the job he'd been sent in to do, and he'd not discovered what was happening with the young women until he'd been in deep cover for over eighteen months. He'd been stuck, with only two not very good options. His choices: stay undercover and turn a blind eye to the plight of the young women he wasn't in a position to save, or rescue the handful of women he'd initially discovered, blow his cover and potentially get himself and the women killed in the process of escaping, while ruining eighteen months of intel, and saving a few when there were likely hundreds of future victims hanging in the balance.

Bryan's director had left the choice up to him on every step of this operation, and he'd chosen to stay in deep cover and pursue the possibility of taking down the entire operation, thereby saving dozens and potentially hundreds of young women in the future. But that choice had come at a heavy cost to his soul and peace of mind. His director wrapping his knuckles on the desk brought his mind back to the conversation at hand.

"So, how long are we talking here?" Kennedy wanted to know, not even bothering to argue with him. Bryan was an excellent agent, but he knew firsthand how being in deep cover could affect a man. It had cost Kennedy his wife and children decades earlier, which was one reason Bryan had been his agent of choice. No wife. No children. No significant other of any kind, and his parents already gone from this world.

"I don't know. Maybe forever...I just know I can't go back to being a normal agent again until I get my head straightened out. I'm not even sure how to act like a normal human being right now."

"It takes time to re-assimilate to normal life, Bryan, you know that, and Dr. Carter said you're making good progress, better than he expected." Dr. Carter one of the FBI's special psychologists who worked with agents who'd experienced extreme trauma, been involved in a shooting resulting in a death, or been undercover for any length of time. He also happened to be allocated to the San Diego office. The man was a genius, and Bryan had met with him the requisite number of times, but they both knew that at this point, only time could make things better. The man had cleared him to return to active duty, and Bryan had remained silent on that issue. This was his decision and no one was getting a vote in the matter.

"Yeah, well that's great and all, but I don't feel it and until that happens, I'm of no use to anyone, including the bureau. I can't forget the things I saw... and did, and until I can come to terms with those issues, I'm no use to anyone."

Kennedy watched him closely, then sighed and shook his head, "I actually agree with you."

"I need some time to work through things, and now that the trial is over, I can do that."

"And you plan on doing this where?"

Bryan gave him a lopsided grin, "I haven't gotten that far yet." He'd just made this decision on the drive over from the courthouse, but he was certain of one thing. He needed to get away from San Diego; away from anyone and everything that might remind him of what he'd done and given up over the last two years.

Kennedy nodded and then asked, "Any preference for locale?"

Bryan shook his head, "Somewhere quiet where I can get some rest would be ideal."

Kennedy nodded his head again and then picked up his phone and placed a call, "Is Castle Peaks open?" He listened and then nodded once, "Good. Mark it off the available list indefinitely. I'll let you know when it's open for business again."

He listened again and then responded, "I don't have the answer to that right now. For the time being, just de-list it. Not for sale, not for company business... treat it as if it doesn't even exist. And if that photographer becomes a bigger problem, let me know. I'll make sure he has more pressing matters to deal with."

He hung up the phone and then met Bryan's inquisitive eyes, "Go see Samuel. He can give you directions to the safe house up in Castle Peaks. It's yours for as long as you need. And Bryan, if you decide you can't do field work anymore, I'll understand. I won't like it," he told him with a grin, "but I'll deal with it. I can always use people behind the scenes."

Bryan didn't comment, he simply nodded, "Castle Peaks?"

"Montana. There's a safe house up there we've used in the past, but was targeted to be sold off before year end."

"Since when does the FBI get rid of safe houses?" Bryan asked, not having ever known that to happen before.

"We don't normally, but a wildlife photographer stumbled across this one several months ago, and it showed up in several mainstream publications. When people started digging around to find out the name of the owners, it got traced back to the feds and speculation rose. For now, the records show it is part of a property dispersal being handled by the Department of Justice, and the records are sealed."

"I thought most of our safe houses were hard to find."

"They are, and this one is, too. It's also one of the most elaborate wilderness safe houses in that region of the country. It was set aside decades ago as a hideaway for high ranking officials, including the President of the United States. You either have to be very lucky, or know where you're going in order to even find it.

"Go see Samuel as he's been there, and he can give you directions and the information you'll need to get along with everyone in the town. His wife is actually from there, so she can maybe give you some pointers on how to fit in."

"You make it sound like I'm going there for the social life..."

"No, but I do expect you'll need to interact with the townsfolk from time to time, for groceries and things, and this is a small town. If you don't have a plausible reason for being up there and make an effort to be involved at least a little, it will only draw more suspicion to your presence."

"Do the people who live there know about the safe house?"

"Most of them think an eccentric billionaire owned the property and was so paranoid about the Soviets that he located the cabin deep in the woods so he couldn't be found. A handful of people know the truth, the Sheriff and his wife being two of them. I'll instruct Samuel to let the Sheriff know you're headed his way. "

"Well, it sounds isolated, which is perfect for now. As for interacting with the townsfolk, I'll keep that to a minimum. I'm not feeling real social at the moment."

"Whatever. Go get yourself together and if you need help, you'd better be asking. I can have Dr. Carter up there in a flash."

"I won't need him, but I'll keep that in mind."

"See that you do. We'll talk again in a month and go from there."

Bryan nodded and headed back to his own desk. He filed the appropriate paperwork and left the office. Half an hour later, he was slipping into his cherry red Corvette and headed for the coast. Samuel Drackett and he had been agents together for years. Samuel had been the first person he'd seen upon returning to the San Diego office after the cartel raid, and had known he would need a place to decompress after all the legal stuff was finished. Samuel had offered his beach house, saying he and his wife were rarely there and wouldn't mind a houseguest, and Bryan had intended to take him up on the offer for a few days while he figured out what came next. Now it looked like he wouldn't need to inconvenience them that way. He could go lick his wounds and let his soul heal, if that were even possible. An out of the way place in the middle of nowhere sounded great. He'd never been to Montana, but from what he could tell, it was a fairly isolated spot with only a small town nearby. Exactly what he needed right now.

He headed for Samuel's house on the beach, arriving thirty minutes later with a sigh of relief. He slipped out of the car, but instead of heading towards the house, he walked around the side and took the stairs down to the beach. Samuel was there, about thirty yards ahead of him, walking along the beach and holding the hand of his new wife. Lucky was running in the surf, no doubt chasing a stick Samuel had thrown for him.

He paused at the base of the stairs and just watched the new family. Bryan had missed out on many things while undercover, and Samuel's wedding was one that he truly regretted. He'd only met Jane twice, and each time she'd fed him something fabulous. *Samuel was one lucky man!*

Pushing aside the twinge of jealousy, he strode towards them, lifting a hand in greeting and then bracing himself as Lucky spied him and raced across the wet sand to offer a doggie greeting.

"Hey, Lucky. Good boy!"

Samuel and Jane joined him, "All finished?"

Bryan nodded, "Yeah. Kennedy and I talked...I'm taking some time to get my head straightened out and figure out if I can still do this job." *To figure out if I still want to do this job.*

"Sounds good. You still want to stay here?" Samuel asked in his quiet way.

Bryan shook his head, "No. Thanks though. Kennedy arranged for me to use the safe house in Castle Peaks. I can stay there as long as I like, and that way I won't be putting you guys out. He said you could give me directions?"

Samuel nodded, "If he's sending you up to Castle Peaks, you'll want to meet Jane's cousin Trent. He's the local sheriff and someone I've known for years. You might remember him too, actually. He trained at Quantico, but decided he didn't want to deal with the politics involved."

"So, what? He just quit and gave up?" Bryan asked, his memory trying to remember anyone who had tapped out during their first few weeks of training at the FBI training academy in Virginia.

Samuel huffed out a laugh and Jane smirked, "Yeah, giving up and quitting—not in this man's vocabulary. No, he decided to downsize, and right after graduation, he turned in his resignation. He didn't want to get assigned to a field office and then feel like he was letting anyone down. He returned to his hometown and was elected sheriff."

Bryan looked thoughtful, "Are you talking about Trent Harding?"

"Yeah, glad you remember him."

"I think I remember the director's reaction more than the man himself. If I remember correctly, no one was very happy with the way things worked out."

"Not in the short-term, but I believe they've come to re-think that. Over the years, Trent had proven to be a valuable resource, living in such an isolated place with a safe house directly under his watch. They even let him use it from time to time."

"Interesting." Bryan gave a tired sigh, "Days like today make me wish I'd done something similar. This case...it took more than I would have willingly given had I known then what I know now."

Samuel nodded and clapped his hand on Bryan's shoulder, "I'll let him know you're headed his way. The safe house is hidden away, but he can see that you get settled and all. Things will get better, you'll see. When were you thinking of leaving?"

Bryan sighed, shrugging his shoulders, and then made a quick decision, "Tonight. My stuff is still in storage and I've got what I need in my trunk already."

Jane shook her head, "Gosh Bryan, that's a long drive. Why don't you stay here for the night and head out early in the morning?" When he looked uncertain, she added with a smile, "I'm cooking tonight."

Bryan laughed, "Well, in that case, how can I say no? Leaving in the morning sounds just fine."

Jane patted his arm and headed for the house, with Bryan keeping pace with her, "You're going to love Castle Peaks. It has the cure for whatever ails you, including a broken and battered soul. I know about this firsthand. If you need space to heal, that's the perfect place." She gave her husband a soft look and then added, "The safe house has also got a special place in my heart."

Bryan raised a questioning brow, "How's that?"

Jane stopped and waited until Samuel caught up to them, "It's where we spent our honeymoon."

Bryan looked at Samuel and shook his head, "You took your new bride to a safe house for your honeymoon? Classy," he joked sarcastically. He shook his head, "Man, I thought you had better taste than that."

Samuel laughed, "Wait until you see the cabin and then I'll be expecting an apology. The safe house in Castle Peaks is something special. Not your ordinary place at all."

"That goes for Castle Peaks in general. The people there are special as well." Jane got a mischievous look on her face, "And who knows, you might find the answer to all of life's unanswered questions residing there. Castle Peaks is full of surprises."

"It sure did the trick for me," Samuel commented with a chuckle, as a broad grin swept across his face.

Bryan nodded his head as he watched Samuel sweep Jane up into his arms and climb the stairs, as Lucky bounced around his legs. They were so much in love it was hard to miss, and also hard to fathom. But not hard to dismiss as a possibility for himself. What they shared was exactly what he'd always hoped to find, but his life had taken so many unexpected twists and turns he was so jaded now and had just about given up hope of ever finding someone he could connect with on such a deep and personal level. Love might be in the cards for others, but so far, it didn't look like it was going to be there for him. *Love is for people who aren't damaged. Guess I should get used to being alone.*

Chapter 1

Castle Peaks, Montana, First week of November...

Jessame Marshall, Jess to those she chose to befriend, walked quickly down the hallway of the Mercer-Brownell Foundation Clinic. She tried hard to keep the skip out of her step, but failed miserably. At 5'4" in height, skipping more often than not resulted in her being seen as a teenager, rather than a mature and competent nurse.

Right now, she couldn't have cared less. She was headed to give Taylor Crenshaw and her parents the news of her latest medical tests. A clean bill of health!

Normally, the attending physician would deliver such news, but Jess and Taylor had struck up a unique relationship during the eight weeks the younger girl had been a resident at the clinic. She viewed Jess as an older sister, and Jess had fallen in love with the younger girl's optimistic outlook on life, especially when she'd come to the clinic with a less than favorable prognosis. One that had since turned completely upside down.

She pushed into the room and stopped, watching as Taylor finished smearing blue finger paint across the piece of canvas that had been stretched across the wall of her room. In an effort to help keep their younger patients' spirits up, Sara Harding – the director of the clinic, had made sure there were plenty of activities to help their youngest patients feel and act like normal kids.

The clinic was a non-profit medical facility that specialized in the treatment of cancer using traditional medicine with a healthy dose of naturopathic and homeopathic treatments thrown in. They'd had remarkable success in the few years since the clinic had been opened, and had just completed the second phase of their expansion project—a clinic specifically designed for kids.

Jess had come to the clinic from Florida. She'd been working at a small hospital along the Eastern Coast of the state when she'd met Claire, Bill Mercer's daughter. The clinic was partially named after Claire's late mother,

Miriam, who had died from pancreatic cancer three years earlier. The Brownell name came from the young woman Claire's father had befriended right before his wife passed away. Sara Brownell had wandered into Castle Peaks, physically ill and running from her new husband after finding out he wasn't the man she'd thought he was.

In a whirlwind romance, Sara had fallen in love with the town sheriff. When she offered to try acupressure to help alleviate some of Miriam Mercer's pain, her success had prompted Bill Mercer and his dying wife to start a non-profit clinic in the hopes of helping others. Sara's own mother had died from cancer, and she'd gladly accepted the position as director of the clinic. While she didn't actually treat any of the patients, she acted as a manager in all other areas and kept the facility running smoothly. She also was the go-to person if you wanted to get something done quickly.

Jess had been intrigued by the concept of the clinic, and after hearing about the pediatric side being built, she had called and scheduled an interview over the phone. Sara had been excited to hear from her, since Claire had already called and provided a great personal reference. Jess had been offered the job immediately. When she'd questioned Sara's ability to make medical staff decisions herself, offering to submit to another interview with others if necessary, Sara had laughed and told her that so far, she'd not made any hiring mistakes and she had a good feeling about this one.

At the age of twenty-five, Jess didn't have a ton of experience, but she was eager to learn and desperate to get away from Florida. She'd done her best to keep that aspect out of her phone interview, but the relief she felt upon receiving the job offer was huge. For almost five months prior to leaving Florida, she'd been harassed by an anonymous stalker; a stalker the authorities had never been able to identify. She'd been receiving eerie phone calls, had discovered notes left on her doorstep, and even stranger gifts had seemed to materialize out of thin air at her workstation at the hospital. She had initially passed it off as a crush that would go away when she didn't react, but that had only seemed to make her stalker more persistent. Just before she'd made the call to Montana, the threats had taken on a decidedly dangerous and threatening tone.

She'd reported each incident, and hospital security had been notified as well, but her stalker was smart. No fingerprints had ever been recovered, and

Jess had started living with a deep-seated fear just below the surface of her psyche. She became nervous and jumpy, and mentally exhausted. A bad combination when you were a nurse who worked with critically ill patient's for long hours, sometimes around the clock.

The detective assigned to her case, Walter Broomfield, had suggested she think about leaving town, and prior to meeting Claire, the idea had seemed preposterous. She'd been a Floridian all of her life, but given the choice between living by the ocean and continuing to deal with her unknown admirer, or moving to a place she'd never been before and living in peace, she'd chosen the latter when the opportunity arose. Castle Peaks, Montana.

A more out of the way place she'd not been able to imagine. The small town was one of those places she'd only read about, and never truly believed actually existed. Everyone seemed to know everyone else, and privacy was in short supply among the townsfolk. Jess had thought she might get lonely in such a small place, but just the opposite had proven true. She kind of felt like she belonged there already, even though she'd only been in the area for a relatively short amount of time.

People knew her by name and always offered her a warm smile when she met them at the post office, the church, the drugstore, or the small diner. She was still trying to piece together all of the familial connections, and had made a comment about being a little confused the week before, not realizing Marsha had been listening right around the corner. She'd laughed and told her to wait a few more weeks until everyone's grown kids came home for Thanksgiving or Christmas, then she would really have just cause to feel confused. Jess had simply smiled and decided she needed to keep a journal or something going forward so she didn't offend anyone by forgetting their name or which family they belonged to.

Thinking about families, her current errand was one of the perks of her job at the clinic. Letting a family that had come face to face with the potential death of a child know they had come out the other side victorious had to be the greatest thing ever. *Cancer.* It was the worst word in the English language, or any other language for that matter, because it seemed almost always accompanied by the words death, funeral, and heartbreak.

But not today! This time, the doctors, nurses, and modern medicine had won! She did an imaginary victory dance, barely controlling the urge to do a little jig right there in the doorway to the room. *You're supposed to be an adult here, pretend to have some control over your emotions at least.*

Clearing her throat, she caught the attention of Clarice Crenshaw. She smiled to alleviate the unspoken fear and worry in the other woman's gaze and then nodded towards Taylor.

"Great painting! I doubt Picasso could have done better," she told the young girl, watching as she turned and waved paint covered hands around.

"Miss Jess! Picasso painted weird looking stuff." Taylor turned back to the wall and cocked her head from side to side, "Wow! My stuff doesn't look much better, does it?"

"Beauty is in the eye of the beholder," Clarice reminded her daughter with an indulgent smile. "Why don't you wash up? I believe Miss Jess is here with some news."

Taylor looked back at Jess, and when she nodded, she hurried over to the sink in the corner and began to wash paint from her hands and forearms.

"Are the tests back?"

Jess waited until she turned the water off and then nodded with a smile.

"Yes, the tests are back. Dr. Jackson said everything looks wonderful and you can go home anytime you'd like."

Taylor let out a girlish scream and threw herself into Jess's waiting arms, "Thank you!" She turned to her mother next, "We get to go home!"

Jess watched the pair hug and then added, "Your immune system is still kind of weak so he wants you to ease back into your normal routine, but there's no reason you can't start going back to school. Maybe half days to begin with?"

Clarice nodded, tears running down her cheeks, "That sounds wonderful. We need to call your father and tell him the good news. He was going to drive up here tonight after work, but now he can just come get us and drive us back home."

Taylor nodded her head and then looked around, "Where's Dr. Jackson?"

Jess smiled, "He's waiting for you in the cafeteria, and he said something about celebrating with ice cream sundaes." Whenever one of their patients beat the big "C," the word *cancer* not being spoken aloud if it could be avoided, the entire facility celebrated in one form or another. It might be a cookie decorating party, a visitation from a favorite cartoon character, or...as in the case of Taylor, and ice cream sundae party.

Taylor nodded and then grabbed her mom's hand, "Come on! We don't want the ice cream to melt."

Clarice laughed and allowed herself to be pulled from the room. Jess shook her head and then looked up when she heard soft laughter.

"Oh, Tori. I didn't see you there."

Tori looked back at the happy girl and mom, then smiled, "That's why we do what we do. It never gets old."

Jess nodded her head, "I'm so happy for her. She's a great kid and deserves to live a normal life."

Tori stepped back and Jess followed her into the hallway, "Were you looking for me?"

Tori nodded, "I was wondering if I could get you to cover the walk-in clinic for a few hours this afternoon and evening? I haven't been feeling all that well, and Jackson has decreed that I need a night off." Victoria was a registered nurse who'd fought her own battle against breast cancer and won. She was married to Dr. Jackson, the clinic medical director, and she had a young daughter as well. She'd been a great help to Jess when she'd first arrived, knowing firsthand how difficult moving to a new place, let alone such a small and isolated one, could be.

Jess nodded, "Of course. I'm happy to do it." She gave her friend a quick once over, noting that she looked pale and like she'd lost a bit of weight, "Do you have a bug or is it something more?"

Tori made a face and shook her head, "Honestly, I don't know. I even pulled my own blood, but my white cells were in the normal range. I just feel tired and run down. My stomach's been giving me some trouble lately as well. One moment I can't stomach the thought of food, and the next moment I feel ravenous."

Jess gave Tori a once over with a clinical eye, "Maybe you just have a touch of the flu?"

"Maybe, but either way, I don't need to be seeing patients or worrying Jackson."

"I agree." Jess thought of offering to pull another blood sample and have the in-house lab run some more tests, but she held her tongue. Tori was an excellent nurse and married to a doctor; if there was something wrong with her, she definitely didn't need a younger nurse pointing that out.

"Great! It's normally real quiet, and you can shut the doors down at 8 o'clock and go home."

"Not a problem. I haven't done any sort of triage work since my internship, this will be fun."

Tori shook her head, "Well, I don't know about the fun part, but hopefully it will be quiet. Quiet is always a good thing."

Jess didn't disagree with her, but she actually liked being challenged and kept busy. It was partly why she'd chosen oncology as her specialty—it was always a challenge. She finished her regular shift, grabbed a sandwich in the cafeteria and then headed downstairs to the small walk-in clinic.

Castle Peaks didn't have a hospital, or even an emergency clinic, so when the oncology clinic had been constructed, a small triage clinic had also been added to provide the local citizens with access to emergency medicine in their small town. The citizens were happy and it gave the doctors and nurses working at the clinic a chance to treat patients that weren't suffering the effects of cancer. A win-win situation for all involved.

She grabbed her purse as she headed downstairs, thinking it was a good thing she'd picked up a fresh crossword puzzle book the last time she'd stopped at the drugstore. If it was a quiet night, she might have to pick up another one. Either that, or start playing Solitaire again. Something she hadn't done since nursing school.

The nurse she was replacing at the clinic quickly showed her where everything was, and then they bid each other goodnight and Jess took her place behind the check-in desk. The clinic was only staffed with one person each evening, with the knowledge that additional medical help was only a few minutes away. As she worked her way through crossword puzzle number three, she soon realized that quiet meant boring. Something she did not tolerate well at all. Too much time to think.

She headed into the small break room and heated up a cup of water in the microwave, dropping in a tea bag to steep. The clinic would officially close down in two hours, and as she headed back to the reception area, she found herself struggling to keep awake. She heard the phone ring, and smiled as she answered it.

"Medical Clinic, this is Jess."

"Jess, this is Jeb over at the drugstore."

Jess smiled, "Good evening, what can I do for you tonight?"

"Oh, nothing much. I'm just making a few phone calls to remind folks about the meeting tomorrow night. I just spoke with Tori and she said you were covering for her over there tonight."

"I am. Is the meeting about the holidays?" Jess asked with a smile.

"That'd be the one. I know you're new to town and all, but we'd love to have your help. That is, if you're not too busy."

Jess smiled, "Sara invited me a few days ago, and I originally wasn't planning on attending, but Castle Peaks is starting to feel like home to me. If you don't think people would mind an outsider's input, I'd love to attend."

"The more the merrier, I say." Jeb chuckled and she could hear the bell that hung over the door of the drugstore ring out across the phone line. "Gotta go. See you tomorrow night."

"Yes. Tomorrow night." She hung up the phone, amazed at how a small inconsequential phone call could lift her spirits. She happily went back to finishing her crossword puzzle and sipping her tea, a small smile on her lips, in sharp contrast to before the call when she'd been bored and half asleep.

About twenty minutes before closing time, her cell phone pinged from a number she didn't recognize. The feeling of dread she'd been hoping to escape immediately crawled up her spine as she swiped her thumb across the screen. She felt the blood drain from her face as she swallowed and looked at the message she'd opened. It was from her stalker! Someone she was almost positive had to be male. She was sure of it.

I'm going to find you. You can't hide from me forever.

She immediately activated the screen on her phone that let her block any future calls coming from that specific number and then erased the message off her phone. With shaky hands, she put her phone down on the desk and sat back in the chair.

She'd been receiving text messages from the person who'd begun stalking her in Florida, and only a few months ago, she'd discovered she had the ability to permanently block those numbers from even ringing through to her phone. She'd been advised to change her cell phone number, but she couldn't do that for reasons she couldn't go into with the authorities. So far, she'd been forced to block no less than a dozen different numbers. It seemed her stalker didn't mind getting a new phone to contact her with every few weeks. *But you just received a message yesterday. This person is becoming more persistent.*

She took a calming breath, mentally talking herself down from the panic that threatened to overtake her. The calls were obnoxious and bothersome, but she'd moved far away from Florida and she was sure her stalker had no way of knowing where she was now.

She'd even contacted Walter, the Florida detective who'd originally handled her case, but been told she was doing the right thing and her stalker would no doubt give up after a while. She just had to stay diligent and not take the bait. She'd been advised to alert the local authorities to what was going on, but she'd not done so yet, afraid that whoever was calling might be tied into the police network somehow. If she told Sheriff Harding what was going on, he might do an internet search on her and then her whereabouts could be potentially be discovered. So, against the advice of the Florida cops, she'd decided to pretend nothing was going on and hope her stalker gave up soon.

She closed her eyes and took several calming breaths, trying to find a happy place for her thoughts to reside. The visualization technique was one she used on frightened kids during treatments, and she'd discovered it worked just as well on frightened adults. Jess preferred to act, not react; that meant she needed to be calm and in control of her thoughts before she did anything else. She sat there for a few long moments, and finally got up and headed back into the exam rooms, deciding she might as well spend the time making sure everything was well stocked and clean before heading home.

It gave her something to do, and helped keep her thoughts at bay. It had been a long week, but one that ended on a high note for both her and the Crenshaw family. She wasn't going to let some unwanted communication from a faceless coward ruin things. She had the next two days off, and had been invited to the Harding's for dinner tomorrow night along with several other people to discuss plans for the upcoming holidays. Castle Peaks came together as a community to celebrate Christmas, and while Jess had only seen pictures from the past, she was excited to be a part of the celebration this year.

Jess had volunteered to organize some fun activities for the children who would remain with them at the clinic over the Thanksgiving and Christmas breaks. Their families would be present, as well as healthy siblings, and Jess was determined to see that everyone found something to smile about over the next two months. She loved the holidays and was looking forward to experiencing her first white Christmas. Sara had warned her it would be an eye opener, but Jess was ready for the challenge. She'd even ordered some fur-lined boots from the Internet, something no Floridian would ever think to buy.

As the time to close the clinic arrived, she locked everything up and prepared to head home, doing her best to forget about the text message and the warning it contained. Castle Peaks was now her home, and after several months of living here and finding acceptance, she didn't want anything to mess with the small measure of happiness she'd found. *There's no way whoever is stalking me knows I moved to Montana. They can't bother me here unless I let them.*

Chapter 2

The highway a few miles outside of Castle Peaks...

Bryan saw the sign for the turnoff to Castle Peaks and sighed in relief. His side was aching something fierce, and about a hundred miles ago he'd started to rethink the wisdom of making the long drive to Castle Peaks from San Diego virtually all in one shot. The healing knife wound on his side had started to throb hours earlier, the bucket seat of his car not being the most conducive to having a three-inch cut zigzagging across his hip and lower abdomen.

His injury had been minor when compared to the death blows the cartel members had received during the final raid and ensuing gun fight. He'd even been feeling well enough that he'd gone to the gym a few times for a light workout prior to leaving California. Shaking his head, he admitted that he might have overdone it on his last visit, acknowledging that the throbbing in his side had intensified since that workout. He knew he should have had the doc check out his healing stitches before leaving town. *Too late for that now.*

As he angled his red Corvette towards the lights of the town, dusk had already come and gone and night had fallen quickly over the landscape. The lights of the small town beckoned to him, and he hoped he could get ahold of Trent and find the safe house yet tonight. Spending another night in the cramped confines of his car wasn't on his bucket list.

He'd made contact with Trent before leaving Samuel's house a few days earlier, but he'd been unsure of what day he would arrive. Originally, he'd planned to leave San Diego two weeks ago, but while he'd been relaxing at Samuel's house, his director had tracked him down and told him there was a problem. A problem that required his immediate attention.

Bryan had cringed upon hearing what was being asked of him, but he knew that the longer he procrastinated, the longer it would be before he would get his much-needed vacation. He'd spent the last two weeks meeting with various FBI personnel as they attempted to make sense out of the computer hard drive that had been recovered during the raid. Bryan had been under the impression that nothing was salvageable from any of the computers that had been confiscated, but he'd been wrong. They'd discovered an encrypted drive in Emilio's private office, and they'd exhausted their abilities as far as decoding the password went.

Director Kennedy had been hoping that Bryan could speak with Eduardo, play upon his newfound Christianity, and gain access to the password. Bryan had balked at having to go talk to the young man, but then his director had landed a low blow, asking him to 'think of the women we might be able to recover.' Key information could very well be found in the files on that drive.

Bryan had driven to the prison and spoken to a very humble Eduardo. After an hour, he'd received the password to the drive without a struggle. Eduardo was doing a credible job of playacting his new found repentance as far as Bryan could see, and even after spending an hour in the man's presence, he wasn't entirely sure if his recent salvation was real or just convenient. Only time would tell.

He'd returned to San Diego and spent the next twelve days helping to decipher the various deals and notes stored on the drive. He'd been undercover for three years, and it seemed that most of the business the cartel had done during that time was referenced on the drive in one form or another. Bryan hadn't relished reliving those three years, but he'd done so hoping for a payoff at the end. Unfortunately, there was little to no mention of the women on the drive. Various types of merchandise were mentioned that could have easily been code for different types of women, but they had nothing concrete to go on.

At the end of the second week, the chief analyst had declared they were chasing a rabbit and tabled the hard drive investigation. Bryan had been released to go about his recovery, and he'd gone back out to see Samuel one last time. Jane had encouraged him to see the country on his trip, to take his time, and enjoy himself. Bryan had just wanted to get to where was going and try to forget all of the memories the last two weeks had stirred up and brought back to life. He'd humored Jane by telling her he would probably stop at the end of each day, so it would only take him two long days of driving, with possibly a few hours into the third day as well; when all the while he had no intention of stopping anywhere. He planned to do the entire drive in one continuous trip.

However, driving straight through had proven impossible and he'd spent the wee hours of the night before dozing atop the bedspread in a cheap motel. It wasn't that he couldn't afford more luxurious accommodations, it had simply been the first place he'd come to once he realized he was a danger to himself and everyone else the longer he stayed behind the wheel. He'd been advised to spend a minimum of three, possibly even four days, making the drive. He'd not listened and this was only the end of the second day since he'd left California, bringing him to Castle Peaks several hours and at least one day earlier than most people would attempt.

Seeing that most of the businesses appeared to be closed down except for the small diner and the drugstore, he opted for the drugstore. The lights were off in the sheriff's office, and his cell phone battery was completely dead at this point. He'd somehow managed to break the connector that went into his phone from the car charger so he was unable to recharge the thing without an actual outlet now. *Maybe the drugstore will have a car charger in stock. That would be helpful, but frankly unexpected in a town this size.*

The green and white sign at the edge of town showed the population to be just over sixteen hundred people, and based upon the various modifications that had been made to the numbers, he guessed that number had been changing rapidly of late. He really didn't care, and as he'd never lived in a town this small before going undercover, he wasn't quite sure what to expect. He'd spent his younger years in a small mountain town of about seven thousand people, but this was way smaller than that. He had a suspicion that the rules of small towns were even more magnified as the population declined.

In his role as an enforcer for the cartel, he'd not been in a position to get friendly with the local townsfolk, and in fact, he'd steered clear of them as often as possible. Something told him that would not be possible here, or well-advised. In a town this size, it was to be expected that everyone would know everyone else's business and feel entitled to voice their opinion on the matter. Busybodies were what his mother called them, and he imagined in some small way they were an integral part of this small town.

He parked in front of the drugstore and opened the door, feeling the icy chill of the wind seep through his short-sleeved black t-shirt. He reached for his leather jacket and slipped one arm into it as he moved his legs and pushed up and out of the seat. The searing pain took his breath away and he pressed a hand to his side, frowning when he encountered the wet fabric of his shirt.

"Great! No wonder it hurts like someone just stabbed me." *They did, just a month ago.* He carefully slipped his arm into the other sleeve and then straightened up, clenching his teeth until the pain subsided to a dull ache. He walked to the rear of the vehicle and popped the lid to the trunk, quickly locating the bottle of painkillers he'd not needed for almost a week now, and frowning when he realized there were only two pills left. *Should have thought about getting this refilled before I left California.*

"Well, I wonder if the drugstore can refill an out-of-state prescription without a written order?" he muttered as he closed the trunk and pocketed the pill bottle. He headed for the glass doors and pulled them open, nodding when the warmer air hit his face.

He stepped inside and paused for a moment to take it all in. This was a good old-fashioned drugstore, complete with a soda fountain, jukebox, and even black and white tiles on the floor. An older man stood behind the counter wearing an apron, and had a welcoming smile on his face. He had white hair, and little round wire-rimmed glasses perched low on his nose.

"Good evening. Welcome to Castle Peaks."

Bryan nodded and walked towards the counter, "Thanks. Can you fill prescriptions?"

"Well, now. That all depends. You aren't from around here, are you?" The man peered out the window and his eyebrows raised when he saw Bryan's vehicle.

Bryan shook his head, "No, but I'm going to be staying here for a while. Sheriff Harding knew I was coming, but I'm at least a day or so early." At the mention of Trent, the older man smiled and came around the counter.

"You must be that fellow from California who needs a place to recuperate." He extended his hand, "Jeb Matthews's the name."

Bryan shook his hand, "Bryan Jackson. Good to meet you." His side was throbbing a little stronger and he sucked in a quick breath before releasing it. "You have a bathroom around here I could use?"

"Sure enough, straight back. You're looking a little peaked all of a sudden, is everything all right?" Jeb asked, eyeing him up and down.

Bryan nodded, "I think so. I'll let you know if that's not the case." He headed towards the back of the store and then paused, asking, "Would you mind seeing if you can get ahold of the Sheriff for me? My cell phone battery died and it sounds like I might need his help finding the cabin where I'm going to be staying."

Jeb nodded, "I'll be happy to call him for you. Give a holler if you need any help. You sure you're doing okay? Trent said you'd been injured..."

Bryan nodded his head, "I'll be fine, just been driving for too many hours without a break. Be back in a minute." He headed for the bathroom and shut and locked the door before removing his jacket by letting it slide off his shoulders to the ground. He glanced at his reflection in the mirror and grimaced. His California tan was a pasty gray color, and his deep blue eyes were showing exhaustion and pain.

Looking down, he peeled his t-shirt up to reveal the angry redness of the cut, obviously irritated and showing signs that one of the newer stitches had come loose. It should have healed by now, but he'd developed an infection in it several weeks ago, and now it was like a bad penny and just wouldn't go away. A small amount of fluid had leaked from the healing wound, but thankfully there didn't seem to be any blood mixed in with it. He used a damp paper towel to clean off the wound and then folded one of the dry towels to form a makeshift bandage over the oozing wound.

He picked his jacket up and headed back for the front of the store. Jeb greeted him with a smile, "I got ahold of Trent and he's headed this way. Said it might take him about twenty minutes as he was putting their little one down for the night, but he invited you to either go on over to the diner or just hang out here with me."

Bryan nodded, "If you don't mind, I'll just hang out here for a bit." He slid onto a bar stool and then scanned the small store, "You don't happen to carry basic first aid supplies around here do you?"

Jeb nodded, looking concerned, "I carry a few, but the clinic just up the street has a much better selection. What are you needing?"

Bryan lifted his shirt and removed the makeshift bandage, "Like something to cover this up?"

Jeb's eye's widened, "Wow, that's a nasty looking cut you've had there." Jeb peered at it a bit closer, then picked up the phone before Bryan could say anything else. He dialed a number and then waited for a moment, "Jess, don't mean to be bothering you again, but I've got me a visitor over here who could do with a little medical attention if you were of a mind to help a stranger out."

Bryan tried to get the man's attention to tell him he didn't need the help of whomever had just been summoned, but Jeb just pretended not to see him. He nodded his white-haired head and then spoke again, "He'll be here for a few minutes. Stop on by on your way home. I think your basic kit should suffice."

Jeb hung up the phone and then met Bryan's gaze, "Now, I know you probably don't want to be a bother to anyone, but Jess was covering over at the clinic tonight and was just getting ready to head home. Stopping by here is no problem. Jess'll get you fixed up, or call Dr. Baker or one of the clinic docs if needed. You couldn't be in better hands."

"I don't really think I need medical assistance. I overdid it at the gym a couple of days ago, that's all."

Jeb shook his head, "Can't be too careful with a wound like that, and you don't want to start your vacation here by feeling poorly. Like I said, Jess will get you all fixed up. As for that prescription you were asking about, if you tell Jess what it is you're needing, I'm sure someone here can get you a script that can be filled quickly."

Bryan shook his head, feeling like he'd just been steamrolled, but he wasn't in a position to refuse the help that was being offered. He was in a strange town, and although he knew Trent from the past, it had been a number of years since they'd seen one another and he didn't want to make any assumptions. He was at the mercy of these people and this town while he tried to get his head and his heart healed up, and it would be more than rude to refuse whatever help was being offered him.

"I don't want to put anyone out, but if you don't think he'll mind, I'd be very appreciative of the help."

Jeb started chuckling and Bryan realized he had missed the joke, "Did I say something funny, or are you normally just this happy?"

Jeb shook his head, "Sorry, I wasn't laughing at you, but..." He broke off as the front doors opened and he grinned broadly, "Well, any explanation I might have made is a moot point now. Jess is here." Jeb tipped his head towards the door and Bryan turned to greet the man, his mouth falling open in shock as the most beautiful young woman he'd ever laid eyes on walked through the door. *Wow! Jess most certainly wasn't a guy...!*

Second Chances Series

Thank You

Dear Reader,

Thank you for choosing to read my books out of the thousands that merit reading. I recognize that reading takes time and quietness, so I am grateful that you have designed your lives to allow for this enriching endeavor, whatever the book's title and subject.

Now more than ever before, reader reviews and social media play vital roles in helping individuals make their reading choices. If any of my books have moved you, inspired you, or educated you, please share your reactions with others by posting a review as well as via email, Facebook, Twitter, Goodreads,—or even old-fashioned face-to-face conversation! And when you receive my announcement of my new book, please pass it along. Thank you.

For updates about New Releases, as well as exclusive promotions, visit my website and sign up for the VIP mailing list. Click here to get started: www.morrisfenrisbooks.com[1]

I invite you to visit my Facebook page often facebook.com/AuthorMorrisFenris[2] where I post not only my news, but announcements of other authors' work.

For my portfolio of books on your favorite platform, please search for and visit my Author Page:

You can also contact me by email: authormorrisfenris@gmail.com

With profound gratitude, and with hope for your continued reading pleasure,

Morris Fenris

Self-Published Author

---

1.   http://www.morrisfenrisbooks.com

2.   https://www.facebook.com/AuthorMorrisFenris/

Did you love *New Beginnings*? Then you should read *John Yancey*[3] by Morris Fenris!

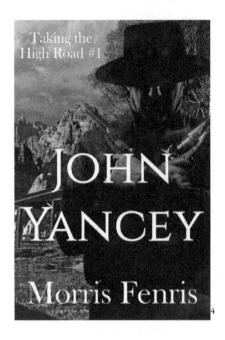

Pinkerton Agent **John Yancey** is hired by Noah Harper to find his half-sister, **Cecelia Powell**, who he claims stole part of his inheritance.

An agent who always gets his man, or woman, Yancey tracks Cecelia to San Francisco, but as he gets to know her, he starts to wonder if his client has been completely forthcoming with him.

But he's contracted to do a job, so he reports to Harper where she is.

Soon Harper arrives in San Francisco from Boston, and Yancey learns who the real villain is.

At the same time, he finds himself developing strong feelings for Cecilia.

"Written in the traditional style of the western with the taciturn, honor-bound hero who protects the weak and punishes evil-doers, this book will delight fans of the western genre."

Read more at https://www.facebook.com/AuthorMorrisFenris/.

---

3. https://books2read.com/u/47KoL4

4. https://books2read.com/u/47KoL4

Morris Fenris
Author

About the Author

With a lifelong love of reading and writing, Morris Fenris loves to let his imagination paint pictures in a wide variety of genres. His current book list includes everything from Christian romance, to an action-packed Western romance series, to inspirational and Christmas holiday romance.

His novels are filled with emotion, and while there is both heartbreak and humor, the stories are always uplifting.

Read more at https://www.facebook.com/AuthorMorrisFenris/.

Made in United States
North Haven, CT
30 April 2022

18746875R00114